AFTER BEFO

K.T. Dady

AFTER BEFORE
K.T. Dady

To my friends who have known both light and shade.

1

Mackenzie

Out of all the families in Willow Tree Street, I believed that my parents had the least talented child. Even thirteen-year-old Rosie Bambridge at number twelve had more talent than twenty-three-year-old me. To be fair, she was some sort of junior ice-skating champion. She was always coming home with trophies. I was fifteen the last time I went ice-skating. I could just about stand up, and George dislocated his finger.

George Wilson lived at number five, opposite me. He was one of my best friends and had been since I was four and he was six, which was when our parents both moved into the newly built street in Oswell.

To me, Oswell was the quietest village in the world. Nothing happened, and no one seemed to care. Why anyone decided to build a new street there, lined with detached houses, was beyond me. There were much livelier places in Norfolk to live.

George went off to uni as soon as he left school, and he came back with a degree in psychology and an upcycled accent. His usual immature, flamboyant personality had taken a hit, and he had taken up jogging. I hardly recognised him.

'It's time to get serious about what you want from life, Mackenzie,' he told me at the time.

The most unusual part of that conversation was the bit where he called me by my full name. Normally, he would call me Mac, like everyone else did, barring my parents.

I decided to have a gap year when I left school, which went on to last forever. My part-time job in the local pub was about as far as I went, much to my parents' silent disappointment. I just didn't see the point of going away to study something when I still didn't know what I wanted to be when I grew up.

I often wondered if people thought I was just thick.

My dad once told me that I just hadn't found where I fitted in this world yet.

Mum always wished I would hurry up and fit somewhere that paid well. Somewhere she could brag about down the post office where she worked part-time.

She didn't have to work at all. My dad earned enough for us all, but she always said that everyone should have their independence. She was fiercely proud of hers.

I had another friend in my street. He lived next door to me. Our houses had a weird L-shape design to them, so our bedroom windows faced each other around the back. We started waving to each other when we were little. As we grew, we would sit at our windows and chat. I would sometimes sit on the ledge with my legs dangling down to the grass between us, if the weather was nice. He would stay seated in his wheelchair. A lot of the time, he would put up poems and pictures in his window for me to see. He was always there to cheer me up.

Adam wasn't like most people I knew. He was introverted and liked to mind his own business. Everyone in my life was the extreme opposite.

I enjoyed the peace and quiet that came with Adam. I always felt recharged after spending time with him.

He was in my year at school, but he never spoke to me there, only at home through the windows. I rarely saw him outside of his house. I knew he worked from home, and I knew it was something arty.

Everyone in my street had something going on in their life, except me.

My gran once told me that we have moments in our life that change us forever.

I would say that my first life-changing moment came when George got me a job interview where he worked.

2

'You want me to work with you?'

George's rosy face dropped. 'Don't say it like that.'

I wasn't trying to be rude. I was just surprised. 'But what would I do at a junkie rehab centre in the middle of nowhere?'

George looked far from impressed by my choice of words about the big posh house where he worked, which was a twenty-minute drive from our village and a lot longer by bus, which only took you part of the way. The rest you had to walk, mostly down a long twining country lane, over a field that had cows in it, and across a small brook, and then through some trees, which wasn't creepy at all.

All of this I found out when going for my interview on Monday at ten in the morning. George would have driven me, but he was somewhere else doing some sort of training day. He may have been good with people, but he wasn't any good drawing maps, and it would have been nice if he had told me to wear wellies.

I arrived at Moreton Hall wearing a grey two-piece suit, which had cropped trousers. I had black loafers on, but they were no longer noticeable thanks to the cow field and the torrential rain that took place the night before, also, the fact that it started to rain again as soon as I hit the trees.

My long dark hair, which had blow-dried rather nicely that morning, much to my surprise, was looking limp and lifeless.

I pressed the white button sticking out of the wall where it said *press* and waited patiently under the shelter of the stone porch, wondering if my mascara really was as waterproof as advertised. I reached into my black leather handbag and rummaged around until I found a tissue.

My hair was dripping, but there really was no need for my nose to be.

The door opened at the same moment I had the tissue wrapped around my finger and shoved up my right nostril.

'Oh, hello.' I quickly pushed the tissue into my jacket pocket and hoped it had done a good clean job. My hand reached out, but I was fully aware that the middle-aged woman frowning down at me in the doorway would not want to shake a hand that had just been up a nose. I lowered my arm.

'I'm Mackenzie Watson. I have an interview at ten.'

A sort of smile appeared upon the woman's face. It was a crooked one that seemed already disappointed in me.

'Come in,' she said.

It wasn't exactly a warm welcome, but I let it go. After all, she worked in a private establishment all day long with rich people probably moaning about how bad their privileged lives were. She had to listen to them telling her what led them down the road of addiction and chaos. They probably thought a few weeks away in a luxurious retreat would cure them and bring them peace. She'd probably had her fair share of the place, and who would blame her.

My part-time job in the pub was hard enough. I often had to listen to drunks feeling sorry for themselves. Probably the reason George thought I'd be a perfect fit where he worked.

George never spoke much about his workplace. Everyone knew it was a private drug rehabilitation centre tucked away from the eyes of the world. There wasn't really much else to say. Plus, he had been made to sign a non-disclosure agreement when he started work. He told me I would have to sign one as well, and to not complain about it, and just sign the bloody thing.

I was only lined up to make tea, coffee, and sandwiches, but all the same, I had to mind my own business, which suited me. I wasn't that much of a people person. I often found people quite draining.

The hallway to the house was huge. It had a lot of dark panelling, a wide stairway, and lots of different ways to go. I imagined a giant Christmas tree standing by the stairs and an open fire crackling away somewhere nearby. It was early autumn, so none of that was taking place, but I felt a strange sense of cosiness standing there trying not to shiver.

The woman led me into a side room. It reminded me of a hunting lodge, not that I'd ever seen one. There wasn't a deer's head on the wall or anything, but it had the kind of walls that normally had one. I bet it did once, before the place became a sanctuary.

'Sit down, Miss Watson.'

I looked at the brown leather sofa behind me that she was pointing at.

'Erm, I'm a bit wet.'

She murmured and sighed deeply to herself. 'Yes, you are. Wait there.'

I watched her leave the room. I removed my jacket and straight away noticed my bra showing through my wet white blouse. Not the best look. I was considering putting my jacket back on when she quickly returned. I awkwardly folded my arms over my breasts as she approached me with a long, fluffy, white bathrobe.

'Take your blouse and trousers off and put this on,' she said casually. She pointed at another door in the room. 'There's a bathroom in there. You can get changed. I'll have someone dry your clothes and clean your shoes.'

It wasn't something I had visualised when I was awake half the night worrying about my interview at Moreton Hall.

I took the robe and made my way into the bathroom, acting perfectly normal.

The bathroom was light, fresh, and clean. It smelled of flowers and had lemon hand cream on the side. I knew it was lemon because I used some after I put on the soft robe. If she served me some hot chocolate when I returned, I had already decided I would work there forever.

I was given a cup of tea by a middle-aged man who came to take my clothes. He radiated a soothing energy, and he had an infectious smile. I thought he looked a bit like Bob Marley.

Dad loved Bob Marley. Every Sunday morning, without fail, No Woman No Cry would fill our house, along with the smell of bleach, thanks to Mum's weekly home sterilisation routine.

I turned back to face the woman as the man with my clothes left the room. Her face lacked a smile. I wasn't sure what she was thinking or what she had planned for me next.

If it weren't for George being the person I trusted most in the world, I would have felt slightly vulnerable. I wished the man who took my clothes was still in the room. At least he had a cheery expression that made me feel instantly comfortable.

'My name is Victoria Huntley,' she said. 'You can call me by my first name. I'm not the owner, but I am in charge here.'

I smiled and sipped my tea. I was sitting on the sofa looking as though I were ill and my mum had just called the doctor out to see what was wrong with me. Victoria Huntley had that doctor look about her and a clear, firm voice to match.

'How much has George told you about Moreton Hall?' she asked.

She was sitting up straight, opposite me. Her perfect posture encouraged me to try to do the same. 'Not much,' I replied. 'He doesn't talk about his work.'

A slight smile appeared in the corner of her mouth. Her cool eyes stayed fixed with mine. She slowly leaned forward and tapped a piece of paper that was on the wooden coffee table between us.

'This is a non-disclosure agreement.'

I interrupted, 'Oh, yes, George mentioned that.'

She paused, as though annoyed with me. 'If you want to work here, you will need to sign it now.'

I wasn't quite sure if that meant I had got the job already. I looked down at the form. A pen came into view. Victoria was holding it in front of my face.

'If you wouldn't mind, Mackenzie.'

She sounded like my old maths teacher.

I took the pen and signed the paper. I could hear George in my head telling me to get on with it. He had already approved it. I knew I wasn't signing my life away. I didn't have a life.

Victoria picked up the paper and browsed it over. Everything seemed to be in order, so she placed it down by her side on the sofa.

'Now I can tell you about Moreton Hall,' she said, her voice losing its sharp edge.

Okay, juicy celebrity gossip coming up. I did wonder if any Hollywood movie stars were upstairs, or maybe a rock star. They were quite well-known for taking drugs at wild parties and ending up in places like Moreton Hall.

I sipped my tea again. It was a decent cuppa. I felt warmer and relaxed, very much at home. I could have easily moved in. I already knew where the Christmas tree would go. I wondered if there was a swimming pool somewhere. Adam would love that. He never went out anywhere much, but his mum made him go swimming every day in the pool in their back garden.

It was a closed-in swimming pool, with glass walls, built not long after Adam had his car accident when we were eighteen. He could no longer use his legs, but that didn't stop his mum from making him exercise the rest of his body.

If I ever wanted to watch him swim, I looked out of my dad's office window. No one was ever invited over for a swim. I'd never been able to swim very well, but there had been occasions where I wouldn't have minded floating on an inflatable lilo while Adam carried on with his lengths.

Adam looked great with his ripped body, but I needed to lay off the cakes, not that I was overweight, just a bit podgy. My dad always said it's good for people to have a bit of podge, just not too much podge, which was the reason he took up jogging around our house.

My dad tried jogging outdoors, you know, like a normal person, but he said the ground was too hard, so jogging around the house was kinder on his knees because of the carpet.

'Moreton Hall isn't quite what people think,' said Victoria, jolting me out of my daydream.

I looked up from my cup.

She threw me a sharp look. 'To the outside world, we are a drug rehabilitation centre. That is a lie.'

She had my full attention.

'We are a rest and rehabilitation home for former members of cults.'

'Cults?'

Victoria nodded slightly. 'You do know what a cult is?'

I nodded.

'Our guests have been through a lot. They haven't all been brought here willingly. Some of them are in great danger, which is why this place is a secret. No one must know of their existence. To some organisations, their old member, our guest, is dead. They are safe that way. We have had guests here in the past who are targets for certain religious leaders. Although, one would hardly refer to those types as religious. These are not your standard religions we are dealing with, Mackenzie. There are many cults all around the world, and some are far worse than you can ever imagine.'

I had read some stories over the years, and seen some documentaries. I knew what cults were capable of.

'Our guests are treated tenderly here. They come from wealthy families, but chose to live a different life. Their families have them back now, and they want them to recover and return home one day. Do you understand?'

Yeah, I was getting it. Rich kids ran away with the circus, then realised they weren't better off.

'I understand.'

She didn't look as though she believed me.

'Your job here will be to serve the meals, and tea in between. Right now, we only have two guests. Claire and Sam. Claire will be leaving us in two weeks. She's ready to go home, and she is one of our safe guests, which means there is no threat outside to her life.'

'How long has she been here?'

'Three years.'

I guess my face said what was in my head.

Victoria nodded. 'Yes, sometimes, it can take years to rehabilitate someone.'

'How old is she?'

'She's twenty-one. She joined an organisation called Wanderers when she was sixteen. She was very young. Her parents hired a private investigator to find her, and another team of people to help bring her here to us.'

'Are you sure she won't just run off again when you let her out?'

'We're sure.'

She looked very sure.

'And what about the other guest, Sam?' I asked.

'Sam's been with us just under a year. He's twenty-three, and he was also brought here by a parent. Sam's life would be in danger if the people of Mindforder ever found him.'

'Mindforder. I've heard of them. I didn't know they were bad.'

'Very bad.' Her eyes drifted away to the large floor-to-ceiling window that looked out to the grounds. 'There are some very bad people out there, Mackenzie. The world can be a scary place.'

I gazed over to the window.

Her eyes quickly came back into focus and stared straight at me.

'You'll start first thing tomorrow, and do take the road next time,' she said, glaring at my feet. 'It's drier, and there are no cows.'

'George sent me that way.'

Victoria almost laughed. 'He would.'

'Do you mean I didn't have to go that way?'

'The narrow road at the top where the bus stops will lead you to our driveway.'

Good one, George, you rat, sprung to mind.

'I've always loved George's sense of humour,' said Victoria, standing up. 'He is a joy to work with.'

‘I’ll give him joy to work with when I see him,’ I mumbled to myself.

‘I’ll just go and see if your clothes are ready.’

I stood up as she left. I walked over to the window to see if the rain had stopped. It still looked a bit drizzly, but it was dry enough.

There was a man walking outside. He had dark hair and a lean outline. A light breeze was blowing gently through his mop of hair. He was wearing navy track bottoms and a matching sweatshirt. He looked cold but uncaring. He stopped and stared out towards a lake. The lake looked as lonely as him. His head tilted to one side, and then he slowly looked over his shoulder, as though he could feel the presence of someone watching him. He turned and looked straight ahead at my window.

I could barely make out his pale face. He wasn’t moving. He was just staring at me.

‘That’s Sam,’ said Victoria, appearing behind me.

3

I was sitting upstairs in an office, which was where all the guests' files were kept. It was my first day at work, and Victoria had told me to start by reading Claire and Sam's files. She wasn't too concerned with me reading Claire's file, as Claire was about to leave soon, but I had to learn about Sam. Everyone who worked at Moreton Hall had to know the guests inside out, which basically meant learning their backstory.

I sipped my cup of tea as I read Sam's confidential file. There were no windows in the room, and the lighting above me wasn't very bright, but I had a desk lamp switched on as well, so I snuggled down under that as though I were about to tuck into a good book.

A couple of pages in, and it did feel as though I were reading a book. This couldn't possibly be true.

There were psychiatric notes inside from the first hospital he was taken to and some more notes from the psychiatrist that visited Moreton Hall once a month. The rest was left up to George, who was a daily counsellor, and Lennie, who was a senior therapist who came once a week, and, as it turned out, was the man who dried my clothes and made me tea.

Judging by the notes, Sam only spoke to George, and even then, he rarely opened up.

George popped his head around the door.

'Oi, Mac. You're supposed to keep this door locked.'

He made me jump.

'Oh, you're back.'

He came inside and closed and locked the door behind him. He plonked himself down in one of the high-back chairs and grinned in my direction.

'What's up with you?' I asked. I pointed at Sam's file. 'You know I'm supposed to be working.'

He ruffled his thick head of mousey hair and continued to grin widely. George had such a soppy grin. Whenever he smiled that way, his bright blue eyes would shine, making them look even bluer.

'I had a great time on my course,' he told me happily.

'Oh yeah, learn anything new?'

'That I'm cute,' he said.

I frowned and tried not to laugh.

'Were you learning or dating?'

'Both.'

I shook my head. 'Who did you meet?' I knew he was dying to tell me. George was an old romantic at heart. He loved love, and he couldn't wait for the day it found him. His eagerness to find his own whirlwind love story did lead him into a lot of quick fix relationships that did little to fulfil his fairy tale dream.

'His name is Lukas. He's two years older than me, and he lives on his own. He is so nice.'

I watched his eyes go all dreamy. 'You always say they're nice.'

He shrugged. 'Well, they are at first.'

'So, how long did it take you to fall in love this time?'

He frowned at me. 'Not sure I care for your tone.' He paused and then grinned to himself. 'The first time he looked at me.'

'Oh, George! You know that's a load of old nonsense. Love at first sight isn't real.'

He scowled my way. 'I'll have you know, Mackenzie Watson, that love happens in many ways, and I should know because I study the mind.'

'Shouldn't that be the heart?'

'Whatever it is, I know it's real.'

'That's because you've fallen in love more times than I can count.'

He let out a big sigh and relaxed into his chair. 'This time I think it is real.'

'Where is he now? Gone home, I suppose.'

He sat up straight. 'We all have to go home, Mac. He does live there, after all. Anyway, it's not far, only London, and he said he will email me.'

'So, you'll have a pen pal.'

'Are you going to continue to rain on my parade?'

I nodded and sipped my tea.

He stood up and took my cup from me. 'You're not allowed food or drink in here.' He drank my tea. 'I'm going to see if Sam will talk to me today, and I'll see you at lunchtime. Hopefully, by then, you will have more faith in true love. Oh, and by the way, how's Adam? My mum said that his mum said that he hasn't been for a swim in two weeks. She didn't say why. You know she doesn't talk much about him. Do you know if he's all right?'

I hadn't even noticed. 'I'll check tonight.'

I had left Adam a sign up the window last night, telling him I had got the job. There wasn't any message waiting for me this morning. Adam would have put up a good luck sign or something, like he did when I got the job at the Dog and Duck. It was a silly sign. A big smiley face with a large hand holding a pint. I didn't really think too much about the lack of window signs over the last few days.

George walked over to the door.

‘Wait, George. Before you go.’ I nodded at Sam’s file. ‘What’s with this?’

George put on his serious work face. ‘That’s just the way it is with most of them, I’m afraid.’

‘How should I act if I bump into him?’ I asked, feeling a bit wary. ‘I mean, should I worry about what I should say? You know I’m no good at that stuff.’

George unlocked the door. ‘You shouldn’t worry about what you would say. You should worry about what he might say to you.’

‘What does that mean?’

‘Let’s just say, he’s not the politest man, but he’s a lot better than he was when he first arrived.’

I looked down at the file. ‘It says here, he tried to kill himself three times in the first six months here.’

George nodded.

I felt quite sad. ‘I had no idea Mindforder could leave a person in that kind of state.’

‘Mindforder wasn’t the reason he wanted to die.’

‘What was the reason?’

George pointed at the file. ‘A woman.’

‘I’ve not read anything about a woman yet.’

‘Oh, she’s in there, but we don’t know that much about her. He doesn’t like to talk about Maggie.’

4

Maggie

His name was Samuel Patrick Thomas Whittington, or something like that. I wasn't paying much attention at the time when he told me. He was just Sam to me. I remember the first time I saw him. He had one of those built chests and tight waistlines that you could almost see beneath his tee-shirt. He obviously liked to workout. He wasn't a muscleman, just fit, toned, and healthy-looking, a bit like a dancer. He was the same age as me. We were edging towards our twentieth birthday.

Our birthdays were one month apart, not that we celebrated birthdays.

He had dark hair, the kind your fingers could run freely through, and his eyes were warm and gentle. They had a softness to them that drew you in. They drew me in as soon as I locked eyes with them.

I had never had, what you might call, a good life. I had no dad, a part-time, mostly drunk mum, and one sister, who I wasn't remotely close to. She was the cold, closed-down type. We lived in a one-bed flat in East London that had never seen one end of a paint brush. The kitchen cupboards were often empty, and we had days without electricity.

I left home at fifteen to move in with my boyfriend. He was twenty-one, charming, and liked all the same things as me. I thought my life was going to change forever. It did, just not for the better. Little did I know the man he really was. Turned out he was a narcissist, a complete nightmare.

I spent the next two years of my life living in a state of fear and confusion. He stripped me of my personality piece by piece every day until the point where I no longer recognised myself. Some days I could hardly breathe, let alone step outside and face the world, not that there was much world for me to see. I hardly went anywhere.

He finally left me for his next victim. I had just turned seventeen and I ended up with another boyfriend just like him, and another one the same after that one left me. I did start to wonder if I was cursed or something. Perhaps my mum hadn't crossed someone's palm with silver, and now I was paying the price.

Things did change for me, eventually. It was when I was eighteen.

It was one day in June, I was on my way to the supermarket when someone handed me a leaflet. I always took them, out of politeness, but they mostly ended up in the nearest bin. This time, however, for some reason, I read the flyer. It basically asked me if I was miserable, lost, and in need of guidance. I ticked all of the above. It invited me to attend a meeting. The address wasn't that far from the high street, so I popped into the centre on a Wednesday morning to find out more.

You see, my years of hell with my ex-boyfriends had shifted something inside of me. I felt more awake, more spiritual. I was searching for something to help me escape the sadness, the madness. The leaflet had something about it that I felt I could relate to, other than the keywords.

Three months after that first meeting, I had left home and moved into one of the villages, which outsiders called a commune. I was the happiest I had been my whole life.

By the time I'd reached the age of nineteen, I was a trusted member of Mindforder, and was chosen to do more at a higher level.

I had never felt so proud of myself. I was walking around on cloud nine. I couldn't wait to get to the Island and be one of the lucky few who help change the world. I was valued. I was wanted. I had a safe home. Mindforder was my family. A place where women were worshipped. We were treated with the utmost respect. I started off a Member, then worked hard and fast to become a Trustee, and then an Angel. That's the title we're given once chosen for the Island.

Sam was a Guard. That was the title for the men chosen to go to the Island. Before that, he told me he was a Student. That's a lower level than Trustee. Men weren't allowed to have higher levels than women. Mindforder stripped men of their entitlement, and lifted women's self-worth.

There were three men and three women in my group. It had to be equal numbers because we had to be paired up. Only male and female pairings were allowed. Sam was given to me. His new job was to be my husband. My new job was to be his controller.

I'd never controlled anything in my life. I couldn't even control my own life. That's how I ended up in a cult in the first place. Typical me. Although, in my defence, I was lonely and looking for somewhere I could call home, and Mindforder was homely, at first.

5

I had a dark cloth bag over my head for the second boat ride. It was a bit dramatic, in my opinion, but who was I to mention that. We weren't allowed to know the location of the Island. No one said why. It was all a bit cloak-and-dagger. I knew it was a beautiful tropical island because I had seen the pictures.

I had thoughts of sword-swinging pirates or drug dealers holding machetes waiting for me at the other end. Wherever the other end was. I visualised Al Pacino and his little friend. My first boyfriend loved that movie. Then, for some reason, my mind switched to a book I had read in school about kids stranded on an island, and how it all went a bit belly-up.

I had a lot to think about while I was being transported over the ocean, blindfolded. I felt a bit queasy from the motion of the waves, but all in all, I had taken the whole journey quite well. My overactive imagination helped keep me distracted.

I had a lot of practice when it came to sitting in the dark. My last ex-boyfriend used to make me sit in a cupboard under the stairs sometimes. I was scared at first, but then I read Harry Potter one day and, suddenly, sitting under the stairs didn't seem so bad.

It had been a long day, and I was tired. It was around five o'clock in the evening, and I was grateful that we had finally arrived. I could feel the heat almost suffocating me under the cloth.

I was carefully led off the small boat and onto a wooden pontoon.

I remained blindfolded for a further ten minutes as I was led on a short walk and then into a cool room. It was a refreshing feeling. I kept my composure, even though I was extremely dehydrated and in need of some sleep. My adrenaline kept me awake. I was filled with curiosity and excitement. I wasn't in a position to faint. That would not have made me a very good Angel. Angels were known for their strength and self-discipline.

Some of the sweat on my face rubbed off against the cloth bag as it was lifted from my head. I took a moment to adjust my eyes.

The room was similar to a registry office, and it smelled like wood. There was a woman standing in front of me, smiling. She was about fifty, with stern brow lines and cool eyes. Behind her were two men, a bit younger and not so stern. Their heads were slightly bowed. They were all wearing casual clothes, neutral in colour and loose and comfortable. Suitable for the heat on the Island.

I could see from the corner of my eye that there was a man standing to my side. I did not turn my head. I didn't look anywhere but forward. I didn't feel it was acceptable for me to start eyeing up the place like I had just walked into a hotel lobby in Spain. I was pretty sure there wouldn't be a sign pointing the way towards the bar and swimming pool. I could just see myself drinking from a pineapple. I really wanted a drink. Water, to be precise. I really needed water.

Two women stood in line behind me, and two men stood in line behind the man at my left side.

The woman at the front spoke. Her voice was clear, and it was obvious that she knew how to talk to a crowd, big or small.

'Welcome to the Island,' she said happily. 'My name is Claris, and I am the Guide here. I'm sure you have all been voice ever since I went to live in the village. I found it helped others to understand me. There were other accents there too, but I quickly noticed that everyone who had a higher job spoke clearly. I felt I had to change myself, if I wanted to get ahead.

'My name's Rob,' said the Keeper.

Keepers were the guards of the Island. They made sure everyone felt protected and that the Island had no intruders. Apparently, news reporters had tried to get on the Island a few times over the years.

Rob had sun-kissed blonde hair. He really reminded me of a surfer. He was friendly and seemed like fun. I thought he would have suited an Australian accent, but he had a well-spoken English one. He had no Bermuda shorts and no surfboard. He chatted to us all the way to our hut. I felt so grateful for him. He helped me feel relaxed.

The hut was exactly that. A beach hut, of sorts. A small wooden house with only three rooms. One bedroom, with an attached bathroom that had basic plumbing, and one living area that had a small kitchen along one side, and a small sofa on the other. The house smelled musty.

I stood in the doorway and looked around to see if it had air-con. It didn't. I huffed to myself as I walked inside, but ungratefulness was forbidden, so I silently reprimanded myself.

'Don't forget to read the rule book,' said Rob, showing Sam into the hut. 'Took me about four months to remember everything.'

Sam walked over to the laminated book sitting on the kitchen side. I was busy staring at the double bed inside the bedroom.

'I'll leave you to it,' said Rob. He closed the door, shutting us inside together.

I heard Sam's voice. 'Are you hungry?'

A wave of embarrassment rushed over me because I knew that he had caught me staring at the bed. I turned to meet his eyes. They were warm and friendly. He held a pleasant look about him.

I had no idea what vibe my face was giving off. I was trying to act cool about the situation. After all, I knew what I was getting myself into. I just thought it would be less awkward.

I cleared my throat. 'I feel a bit sick, to be honest.'

He pulled his lips in for a few seconds and nodded sympathetically. 'From the journey?'

I re-enacted his facial movements.

He glanced over at the toaster, which made me realise we had electricity. The hut didn't exactly scream mod cons.

'How about some tea and toast?' he asked softly. 'Help line the stomach.'

I nodded again and sat down at the made-for-two wooden table over in the kitchen area while he familiarised himself with the kitchen. I thought about his voice as he went about making my food. It was Irish. Soft and clear. He had a well-raised air about him. He seemed further away from home than me. I was curious about his backstory, but I knew we weren't allowed to talk about our past. Only now existed. Only now mattered, which was fine for me. My past could have been written by Stephen King.

He took a glass jug out of the small fridge and a couple of small glasses from a cupboard. The jug was filled with cold water. He poured us both a glass and then grabbed the rule book and sat down opposite me while waiting for the kettle to boil and the toaster to pop. He placed the book down gently upon the table.

'I'm sorry if I get anything wrong to start with,' he said quietly. 'I'll pick it up soon enough.' He glanced over at me. His cheeks were a touch pink. 'I'm a fast learner.'

I was sipping my water. The fresh liquid felt cold, but so good. I wanted to down it in one, but I knew that would hurt, so I put the glass down. 'You'll do fine, Sam.'

I immediately realised I had used his name. I quickly looked down to flip open the book. I swallowed hard. I had no idea how I was supposed to address him. He didn't correct me, not that he was allowed to.

'I'm not sure what to call you,' I admitted, casually flicking through the numerous pages.

His hand slowly slid across the page I was on. 'You call me Sam.'

I stopped pretending to speed-read and looked up at him. There was that warmth in his eyes again. It was interfering with my self-discipline. I wanted to ask the Island why I had got matched with the bloke with kindness and warmth written all over his face. I guessed it was to test my strength. I pulled myself together.

'Could you remove your hand.' I wasn't asking.

Sam did as he was told. He apologised and then went to butter the popped toast.

We had a kitchen full with basic food items, which did make me smile inside. I knew the Island was all about farming our own food and tending to livestock, so it was nice not to have to do much straight away to have access to food.

Sam served me the tea and toast, then sat down at the table again. I noticed he didn't make himself any. I wasn't sure if I had to eat first. The rule book seemed to be glaring up at me, mocking me for not knowing my place. They really should have given us more instructions beforehand.

'Aren't you hungry?' I asked.

He didn't look like he knew what to say. He was being mocked by the rule book as well. He sipped his water.

'You've got to eat,' I said softly.

Being in the Mindforder family had taught me that my rank was much higher than any man's, but I wasn't the type to take advantage of my new powerful position. I knew full well what it felt like to be controlled. I wasn't about to do that to Sam. I could easily manage my position and my husband and that rule book without a power trip. With great power comes great responsibility. I started thinking about Spider-Man.

Sam lowered his head a touch, but his eyes were still firmly locked with mine. 'I need to catch up on the rules.'

I closed the book. 'We'll make a start tomorrow. For now, let's just rest from our long journey, adjust to our new surroundings, and act like a normal married couple sharing some food.'

He gave a hesitant nod.

I pushed the book to one side and moved the plate of toast to the middle of the table.

He tentatively raised one hand and took a slice of toast and ate it, which made me feel instantly relieved and a little less awkward.

'Would you like a cup of tea as well?' I asked, getting up.

He shot up out of his chair, nearly knocking it over. He made me jump. A flashback from time spent with my first ex swept through me. I caught my breath before it started to shake.

'No,' he snapped. His palm was facing me, a warning to stay away from the kettle. 'You cannot serve me.'

I knew that. It just didn't seem like a big deal to make him a cup of tea. I knew it was. I wasn't thinking clearly. I was

I would have had more confidence in my body if it looked as fit as his. I could just see him in the gym, admiring himself. I wondered if he did. He didn't come across as the confident type, but he also wasn't coming across as the shy type either.

There was no way I was going to reveal any shyness. He was below me. I had to hold my stance.

Sam leaned forward and pulled the covers down. He straightened up and waited for me to get into bed first.

I was glad to. I snuggled down and pulled the white sheet up towards my neck as soon as he was lying next to me.

The bed was a small double, so there wasn't much room. I could just about feel the hairs on his arms touching me. I could smell his skin. He had a combination of salty and sweet about him, bit like my favourite flavoured popcorn.

He loosened the covers around him so that his chest was revealed. I wanted to do the same. The air was hot and humid.

I had the urge to turn on my side and talk to him, but I knew it was forbidden, and I think I had already broken more rules than I knew about. I moved my head so that I could see him.

He was staring at the ceiling. Probably fed up that he got me as his wife. Bony, boring Maggie, who didn't know the rules. Some Angel I was. Oh well, it was only day one. I built up my positivity by telling myself that this was just the start of something wonderful, and that I would succeed in whatever was expected of me.

I had dreamed about the Island as soon as I had found out it existed. Now, I had actually arrived. I was a part of it. A part of something meaningful. I was going to help change the world. Mindforder was going to change the world. The world just had to get on board. We knew the way forward.

We knew how you should think and feel. We knew how to make women equal. We knew the truth. We knew how to make the world a better place. I knew it. Sam knew it. Everyone on the Island knew it. I was determined to be the best Angel they had ever had.

It took Rob four months to learn the rules. It would take me four days. I was determined to show them. To show my husband. I wasn't going to be the one who let the side down. No, not me.

Sam's head rolled over towards me. His warm eyes looked gently into mine. I think he was trying to say goodnight, sleep tight, don't let the bed bugs bite. Maybe he was just wondering why I was staring at him. He didn't look angry or even disappointed in any way, not that he was allowed to be.

I tried so hard in that moment not to melt, but my heart was in my throat. I was suddenly a little bit lost in his eyes.

Great! I'd only been in town five minutes, and I was going to get deported for having a crush on my husband on the first day.

6

The Assembly Hall looked more like a church. I expected it to look like a school hall. The small white church looked like it had just dropped in from Kansas, or maybe Ikea. It was built with white wooden planks of wood. A flatpack church sitting on top of a low hill.

Rob had met us outside our house and introduced us to his wife Jenny. She looked like a Sunday school teacher from the 1950s. Rob did most of the talking all the way to the church, which was strange because his wife really should have taken charge during a meet and greet.

Rob told us that we must hold hands when we enter the building and not let go again until we leave. He also said not to stress over any rule breaking because newbies weren't allowed to be punished. Everyone understood it took a good few weeks to learn how things worked on the Island.

I wasn't keen on the word *punished*, but that was the word he chose.

I was sitting at the end of the aisle towards the back, holding Sam's hand. There was only a small amount of air-con inside, so holding hands became sweaty very quickly. I tried hard not to let my hand fidget in his.

A woman, who looked a bit like Claris, appeared at the front upon a platform. She introduced herself to us newcomers. Her name was Rochelle. She looked friendly enough and sounded extremely confident. She gave a motivational speech, and the people around me used their Book of Wisdom to bang gently upon the back of the seat in front of them as a way of clapping her. Rob nodded at us to do the same.

The Book of Wisdom was Mindforder's bible. We had to take the small black book with us whenever we went to assembly.

We read two passages from it out loud as a group, then we closed our eyes and bowed our heads and prayed in silence for five minutes.

All of the newcomers had to stay behind when the service was over. Rochelle had us all sitting up the front.

I could see her face more clearly. She was older than Claris. Her skin looked worn from too much exposure to the sun. Her grey hair looked dried out and in need of a good deep conditioner. She had perfect teeth and a cheerful smile. One that looked like she really meant it from the inside.

Rochelle was our mentor on the Island. She pretty much ruled the roost. She wasn't in charge of everything. That was a woman who lived in the Main House, which was on the other side of the Island to us.

The Main House was where the babies were born and sent off to our villages to help make the world a better place. It wasn't our job to have the babies. That wasn't something I signed up for, so I knew that I would never be allowed over there. Just knowing it existed so close to me filled me with an indescribable amount of pride.

Being an Angel made me an important part of keeping the Island maintained and functional. I was a wife. I had made it to the top. Along with Sam, we would help feed and supply everything for the Main House. That was our duty. Angels and Guards made the sacrifices so that the people living at the Main House wouldn't have to do anything.

The woman who lived there was the founder of Mindforder. She was our idol. Our spiritual leader. Our saviour. She knew the way forward. She knew how to preserve the world. How to make it better. She was rarely seen in public. She was too important to be prancing around making public appearances.

Her name was Judith Bird, affectionately known as Bluebird. She lived with her loyal husband Buddy. They had been married the traditional way before Mindforder was created, then remarried under the Mindforder rules.

Buddy was well-known to everyone. He often made appearances on his wife's behalf because she was so busy saving everyone. He was charming and filled to the very brim with charisma. Everyone adored him. He spoke so highly of women, and he always reminded people that he was only in public view because he was following orders.

I had seen him twice when I lived in the village. He gave wonderful, uplifting, and very funny speeches. I wished I could one day meet Bluebird.

Rochelle gave us a timetable each. From Monday to Sunday, we now knew what we were supposed to be doing and when and where we were supposed to be doing it.

Sam was given a farmer's job, and I was to help govern the workers in the food supply room.

Women weren't allowed to work. We had to supervise, give instructions, and make sure the men were kept in place. We had to take our husbands water at certain times of the day if they worked outside, and we had to fetch them for lunch, which we all had to eat in a big barn-like hall, aptly named the Barn.

Today, we were to be separated and taken to our place of work to be shown around so that we would know what to do the next day when our work officially started.

I didn't want to let go of Sam's hand outside. I felt it slip gently from mine.

I followed Jenny all the way to the food supply room. She was quiet, which didn't bother me. It was a beautiful sunny day, and I was enjoying the tranquillity of the Island. The sun warmed my face, and thoughts of Sam holding my hand warmed my heart. The thought felt so good, I didn't even chastise myself.

'We get monthly deliveries of some stuff,' said Jenny, leading me into a large hut.

I entered and immediately stared in surprise at some tins of peaches sitting on a shelf.

'And we're allowed some sugar here,' she added.

I did a quick scan for chocolate, but didn't see any.

'We have medical supplies as well,' she added. 'I'll show you where the Ward is afterwards. It's important to know where that is in case you ever need medical attention. We have one doctor and one nurse who work there, and four people who work in the medical supply room. I've never been admitted to the Ward myself, but I once saw a man being taken there.'

'What was wrong with him?' I asked. I hadn't had any vaccinations for the Island, and I started to wonder if it was possible to catch some sort of tropical disease.

Jenny shrugged and shied her dark eyes away from me. She went back to talking about the food supply and how this room was called the Larder.

Jenny made me feel uncomfortable. I couldn't put my finger on it, but there was definitely something about her that didn't sit right.

Another woman came in. She was around the same age as me. She had long, wild, red locks of hair. She had a front cover romance novel look about her. The story would be about a young Scottish girl living in the Highlands, falling in love with rogue men wearing kilts.

Jenny ignored us both and walked over to a small side room to collect a clipboard.

The wee bonnie lass turned my way.

'Hi, I'm Beatrix. I've been here four years now. My husband works over on the farm, which is where I heard they placed yours. Hard work they do over there. Make sure you take water to him. You don't want to get into trouble if he faints from the heat. Make sure he wears his hat. We're responsible for our husbands, you know.'

My shoulders slumped slightly. I was disappointed that she wasn't Scottish. She was English, with a slight Cornish tone in her voice. I nodded at her. 'I know.'

Beatrix nodded towards Jenny. 'Jenny's good with the rules,' she whispered. She looked me straight in the eyes. She paused for a second, then smiled. 'She'll let Rochelle know if any are broken. Read that rule book as fast as you can.'

I did wonder if she was warning me.

Jenny came back out of the small room. She handed me my task sheet and told me it will be the same routine every day, except Sunday, which was everyone's day off.

'Shouldn't you be somewhere, Beatrix?' Jenny said it without making eye contact.

Beatrix gave a sarcastic curtsey. 'Yes, ma'am. I was just leaving.' She grabbed a packet of lentils off the shelf, then signed a piece of paper by the doorway. She gave me a big smile before she left.

I gazed over at two men loading packets of flour into a wheelbarrow. They were to take them over to the Kitchen. They never said a word. They didn't even look up to see the newbie.

'Does Rob do any other jobs around here or is he just a Keeper?' I asked casually.

Jenny shot me a sharp look. 'Just a Keeper?'

I got the feeling I had insulted her.

Her face scowled at me.

'Being a Keeper is a highly demanding job,' she told me flatly. 'Everyone here has one job, and only one job.'

'Are we allowed to change jobs if we want?'

I got another stern glare.

'You have been given the privilege of becoming an Angel, Maggie. Gratitude should be your only thought and feeling.'

'I am grateful,' I said quickly, 'and proud. I was just curious, that's all.'

'Perhaps you should spend your spare time reading the rule book, then you wouldn't feel the need to ask stupid questions.'

She turned her back on me.

That was me told.

* * *

I got back to my hut to find Sam washing in the outside bathroom, which was just a tap and a large metal bowl sitting on a wooden stand.

I stopped and watched him from a close distance.

He was topless and splashing the cold water over his face and chest. He looked like he already had a healthy suntan. I knew I would be red and sunburnt by the end of the week.

I walked down to him, and he stopped and turned to me. The water was dripping from his hair. He looked like he was starring in an advert for some men's hair and body product. He stared in a warm way at me.

I wished he wouldn't.

I walked past him without saying a word because he had given me the hump by looking sexy when I wasn't allowed to think that way about men, especially my husband.

I was the only one with a key, so he was waiting for me to unlock the door.

He followed me inside whilst drying his hair with a white hand towel.

'Have you had a good day, Maggie?'

My brain started to ramble. Not really. I was lumbered with Jenny all day, and she's really weird. Then, I was taken to see our local hospital, and I met the doctor, who had a *I would like to dissect your brain* look about him. I haven't had any lunch and was told I have to run around fetching you water every five minutes in case you faint, and then I'll be in trouble.

'It was all right,' I said. 'How about you?'

I saw his perfect teeth. I wondered if his parents had paid for them to be fixed when he was a teenager or if he just had naturally straight teeth.

'I joined in with some of the work.' He sounded chirpy. 'Got a bit sweaty.'

I can see that, I wanted to say.

'It seems like fun,' he added. 'I'll mainly be on the field working the crops. Tom's wife took us to the back of the Kitchen where we were fed cheese and bread for lunch. That was a fellow farmer I met today. He's showing me what to do. His wife is called Beatrix. She said she met you.'

I nodded.

'She seems nice,' he said softly.

I glared at him. I didn't mean to. I was just hungry and fed up.

He lowered his head. His sprightly vibe was gone. 'I didn't get over-acquainted with her. Honest, Maggie.'

I watched all the happiness drain out of him in three seconds flat. I had done that to him, and I knew how that felt.

I rushed forward and, without thinking, placed my hand on his chin and gently lifted his head so that he was forced to look into my eyes.

'I know that, Sam.' I spoke softly so that he knew I meant my words. 'You're allowed to think someone is nice. Beatrix is nice. You're nice. Please don't feel unhappy. You've had such a good day. I'm just a bit of a grump because I haven't eaten since breakfast.'

His submissive look changed to concern. 'I must feed you, Maggie.'

'It's all right,' I said, but I knew it wasn't.

My stupid mood had completely changed the dynamics of our home, and I didn't like it. Not for one second. A wave of negative energy poured through the hut and filled me with poison. I felt disgusted in myself. What kind of a wife was I? I felt ashamed of myself. I knew within the click of a finger I could make Sam do anything, but I swore to myself that I would never abuse my position, ever. I never did in the village.

'It's not all right, Maggie. Someone should have fed you. It is someone's duty to care for you when I'm away. Someone should be reported for this crime.'

Jenny should have been reported, but as a woman, I knew she wouldn't get in trouble, even if I did tell on her.

'Not today, Sam. Let's just leave it for today. We're new. Let's not make a fuss.'

He did not agree. I could tell, but without saying it, I had just given him an order.

His eyes rolled down to look at my hand still holding his chin. I could tell he wanted me to release him so that he could make me something to eat.

My cheeks flushed as I lowered my hand, and he immediately went to the kitchen and sliced some fresh bread.

'Bread and cheese coming right up for you.' He looked over his shoulder and nodded at the table and chairs.

I sat down and nibbled on a piece of cheese as soon as it was placed in front of me.

He got me some cold orange juice out of the fridge and sat opposite me, watching me.

I thought about those people who were known as feeders. I read a story about one once in a magazine in the hairdressers.

'You don't have to watch me,' I said, mouth full.

I saw him grin to himself as he turned away.

I felt the shift in his energy. He was happy again.

I had never been in control of a husband before. I wasn't sure I was liking it. I didn't want to be a mood changer. I wanted there and then for Sam to feel free. Maybe he already did. He did sign up for this life too.

'I'll get the shower ready for you afterwards, if you like,' he said.

'Okay, thanks.'

'You're not supposed to thank me, Maggie.'

'Sorr…' I stuffed some more cheese into my mouth, telling myself what a crappy wife I was.

I was pretty sure I caught his eyes smile at me.

7

I woke up the next morning and just for a second completely forgot where I was. I wasn't sure of the time. It seemed early.

I quickly realised that the time wasn't my main concern. Sam was. He was spooning me. His whole naked body was pressed up against mine, and his arm was draped over me.

I daren't move. I tried to control my breathing. I wondered if his eyes were open. I didn't want to turn over and look. His breathing seemed relaxed. I rolled my eyes down to look at his hand. I felt awkward, trapped, and weirdly happy.

Then, I sneezed. I felt my face flush and my heart race.

Sam stirred. I watched his arm tighten around me.

I did exactly what I told myself not to do. I turned over to face him.

His eyes slowly opened and looked into mine.

It took a couple of seconds for him to process the situation.

He shot backwards. 'Oh, no, Maggie. I'm so sorry.'

I grabbed the sheet and quickly pulled it up to cover my chest as he leapt out of bed like it was on fire.

He stood there, in all his glory, staring at me with a complete and utter look of horror washed across his beautiful face.

He quickly grabbed some cotton shorts from a drawer and put them on as fast as he could.

I pulled my lips in, as I was sure I was going to laugh. He did look comical, but I knew the seriousness of the moment. I knew how much trouble he would be in if I told on him. I knew it had taken him a long time to build up trust in Mindforder in order for him to become a Guard. I knew I had the power to strip him of his title and send him packing.

His hands faced me apologetically. ‘I’m so sorry, Maggie. It wasn’t intended.’

I sat up. It was time to get serious. ‘It’s okay, Sam. I know you didn’t mean it.’

He sat down on the end of the bed. He lowered his head in shame and swept one hand through his mop of hair.

‘This has to be reported,’ he said quietly.

I shuffled a little closer to him. ‘No, it doesn’t.’

He turned sharply to face me. ‘Yes, Maggie, it does.’

I shook my head. There was no way in a million years I was telling anyone about what just happened.

‘Sam, I don’t want us to be known as the newcomers who get everything wrong.’

He stared at me in silence.

I swallowed. My throat was dry. ‘I know I’m committing a crime by not reporting you, but I don’t think it’s fair to report someone for something they didn’t know they were doing. You were asleep.’

He nodded slightly.

‘I woke first,’ I added, before he had a chance to speak. ‘I didn’t say anything. I turned to face you.’

He remembered. Warmth was in his eyes as they briefly looked down at my mouth.

‘I’m more to blame,’ I told him.

He stared at his hand resting on the bed. ‘I’ll try to be a better husband,’ he whispered.

I felt a sudden surge of hate towards the Island.

* * *

Tom knocked on our door at ten to nine. Sam opened it, and Beatrix walked straight past him and over to me. I was just putting my shoes on, getting ready to walk Sam to work. It was my duty.

'Don't forget to wear your hats,' said Beatrix.

I looked over her shoulder at Tom. He looked about ten years older than her. He had wiry blonde hair and bright blue eyes. I imagined him in a suit selling mortgages and loans. He was wearing loose clothing and a floppy, wide-brim, beige hat. He looked down at his feet when he saw me staring at him.

Beatrix handed me a similar hat from the table and nodded sideways at Sam.

She left the hut and told us to hurry up. Work started at nine, and it didn't pay to be late.

It wasn't their job to guide us to work, but they volunteered to be our guide for the first day. After that, it was up to us to find our way around and turn up on time.

Sam followed me outside. He closed the door and locked it, then handed me the key. I put it away in the front pocket of my apron-style dress.

Beatrix and Tom had started to walk off in front. Tom was one step behind her and slightly to her side. I knew Sam would follow me too. We couldn't get that wrong. We couldn't get anything wrong in public. Someone else would report us if we did. We wouldn't get a choice then.

I turned to Sam and placed his hat upon his head. He kept his eyes on the ground. As I turned to walk away I heard him say, 'Thank you, Maggie.' His soft voice melted my heart.

* * *

The crop field was huge, and men were scattered all over it. I counted about twelve. Tom took Sam to a hut to pick up tools, and Beatrix introduced me to the woman in charge of the workers there.

'This is Maggie, Sam's wife. She'll be over in the Larder. Maggie, this is Mary-Lynn. She's the boss here.'

'I don't like to use the word boss,' said Mary-Lynn.

'Well, you are,' said Beatrix.

I looked at Mary-Lynn. I took an instant dislike to her simply because she reminded me of my mum. She had the same hard face, the same cold tone, and the same empty energy. The only difference was Mary-Lynn was quite muscular.

'Pleased to meet you, Mary-Lynn.'

She nodded at me. 'I hope your husband's not lazy.'

Beatrix gave me a serious look. She was standing behind Mary-Lynn so that the stern woman couldn't see her face. I felt like she was trying to tell me to choose my words carefully.

'He's not,' I said confidently.

'We'll see,' she murmured. She nodded over to a tap coming out of the hut's wall. 'When you come to water him, use that.' She glared at my beige dress. 'Where's your cup?'

Beatrix stepped forward. 'We're picking one up right now from supplies.'

Mary-Lynn looked far from impressed. 'If you don't come back with one, he won't get a drink. Understand?'

I nodded as Beatrix grabbed my arm in hers and said, 'Yes, she understands.'

Beatrix led me over to our husbands, then released my arm. She spoke quietly to Tom, then turned to me. 'Tell Sam you'll see him every hour on the hour to water him until lunch.'

Sam was standing right behind me. He heard every word, but Beatrix gave me a nod that directed me to repeat her words.

I turned to Sam and told him what he already knew.

'I'll see you soon,' I added quietly, as I was sure Mary-Lynn's eyes were boring into the back of my head.

Sam gave a slight nod without making eye contact, and then he left with Tom.

Beatrix took my arm in hers and led me away. She checked over her shoulder often as we walked along the path that led to the Larder. She seemed paranoid.

'When you get your cup, you grab some string too,' she told me. 'You keep it tied to your belt. See, like mine.'

I looked down at her brown skirt to see a plastic white cup hanging from a thin piece of rope that was tied to her belt.

'Can't we just leave the cups back there?' I asked, looking over my shoulder at the way we had just come.

'No,' she replied. 'If someone else loses theirs, they'll take yours. Then, your husband will be the one without a drink, and you'll be up on a charge if he passes out in this heat.'

'Surely, you'll get reported if you steal from someone here.'

She shook her head. 'Not if there's no proof, you won't. You keep your wits about you, Maggie. Nobody wants to be punished here, and everyone will do their very best to make sure they're not, and if that means throwing you under the bus, they will.'

There was that word again, *punished*. Back in the village, no one was ever punished. You got into trouble if reported, maybe demoted, even asked to leave if it was really bad, but I never saw anyone get punished. There were some stories, but they were just from disgruntled ex-members making false reports about Mindforder. We were taught not to listen to them.

8

Beatrix introduced me to two more women in the Larder. Jenny wasn't around to order everyone back to their positions, so the ladies were taking full advantage of her absence.

'It's not like she's the boss around here anyway,' said Beatrix, with one eye on the door. 'She's no higher than us.'

'She just thinks she is,' said Lucy.

Lucy was early thirties, blonde, tall, and very thin. She had a pale, gaunt face that really did look out of place on a sunny island in the middle of who knows where. She spoke well and held a nice posture. She just looked worn out, like her soul was locked inside a box and couldn't breathe properly.

I remembered when I had a look like that.

The other woman standing with us was Annie. She looked healthy and happy. She had dark skin and those cheerful, round cheeks that babies have. I liked her straight away. She had friendly eyes. The type that cared about everyone.

'Jenny just likes to make sure the Island is run well,' she told me.

Beatrix rolled her eyes. 'We all want that, Annie.'

'It's all Eliza's fault,' said Lucy. 'Everyone has been policing everyone since she messed up, and Jenny is the Chief of Police.'

'Who's Eliza?' I asked.

They all hesitated to speak.

Beatrix checked the door again. 'She was one of us until recently.'

Lucy whispered, 'She was taken up to the Main House.'

The women were speaking quietly, like they were forbidden to say.

'She broke the rules,' said Annie.

Lucy nodded. 'She fell in love with her husband.'

'They took her away?' I asked.

They all nodded at me.

Beatrix leaned in closer to the circle we had all formed. 'She tried to kiss him. Obviously, she wanted more than that.'

Lucy nodded in agreement.

I was curious. 'How did they find out?'

'He reported her,' said Lucy.

I wasn't expecting that. 'Her husband?'

They all nodded and made a low murmuring noise.

'It is his duty,' said Annie. 'Eliza knew better than to do that.'

Lucy nodded. 'We've all come here to help bring energy to the Island so that the children are born here with the love and light that will strengthen this world. We know how strong we have to be. How disciplined. We can't afford to have weak links messing up the system. We're the most important people in Mindforder. Well, you know, apart from the obvious.'

'Eliza was weak,' said Beatrix. 'Made us all look bad.'

'Negative energy,' said Lucy. 'No good for the Island. No good for the babies.'

'She just wasn't right for this kind of job, that's all,' said Annie.

Beatrix frowned at her. 'You're being too kind, Annie. We have Jenny on our backs constantly now because of Eliza. She thinks we're all weak links.'

I was curious about something else. 'What happened to Eliza in the end?'

Beatrix shrugged. 'Deported, probably.'

'And her husband?' I asked.

'He's a Guardian now,' said Annie. 'The one who stands on the right behind Guide Claris.'

Lucy sighed. 'He'll never be anyone's husband again.'

I wasn't sure whether or not to feel sorry for him. Guardians had to live on their own, not speak, ever, and follow Claris around wherever she went. That wasn't the life I wanted for Sam.

I wondered if he would report me. He had every right to. I did break a lot of rules. Not telling on him wouldn't go down too well if anyone found out.

I knew there and then that I had to get a grip, pull myself together, and get on with my job. I was a strong, independent, young woman who had been chosen to bring positive life to the Island. I had done well for myself. I couldn't allow that to just fall away because of a soft touch I had for some man I hardly knew.

I was glad of the chat with the girls. It reminded me of my place. I was a carer of the Island. Mindforder needed me. I couldn't mess up like Eliza. I didn't want to leave. How embarrassing that must have been for her, not to mention her husband. I was not about to bring that level of shame to myself, or Sam. I wasn't on holiday. This wasn't a beach romance. This was my life. One that I had worked very hard to get. Mindforder was my family. These women were my sisters. Sam was my husband. We had a job to do.

My mind was still on Eliza and her ex-husband when Jenny walked in and everyone went about their day. I daren't ask Jenny for any gossip. She'd probably report me just for that.

I spent the next hour sitting in Jenny's makeshift office doing admin work. I couldn't concentrate because of Eliza's story, and my own. Jenny scolded me a few times for making mistakes with the paperwork. I thought only the men were supposed to work. I thought I was a supervisor, but Jenny told me that I wasn't really working, as such, more organising.

I was relieved when Beatrix came to remind me that it was watering time down at the farm.

She made sure my cup was secured to my belt. It earned her a stern look from Jenny, but she didn't care. She led me outside into the blazing heat.

* * *

Mary-Lynn blew a whistle. It made me jump. It also made all of the men stop work immediately and walk towards their wives for their cup of water.

I queued up for the tap behind Beatrix. She filled her cup, turned to me, and said, 'They're only allowed one cup. Don't even think about asking for a refill, and don't trip over because you won't be allowed to get some more. The more disciplined they are, the better for women, and the more energy they throw out to the Island, the better for everyone. Energy creates positivity, and the more positivity around here, the better the quality will be for the babies being born up at the Main House.'

I nodded. I knew how it worked, but still, talk about make you feel nervous about carrying a cup of water.

I could see Sam waiting for me as I walked towards him. I felt like I was balancing on a tightrope, I was that careful.

He had to rest upon his knees to drink from the cup.

I looked around at everyone else while he was doing that. I saw a woman tip out the water in her cup right in front of her husband. She had a cold glare about her face as the water sank into the ground. Her husband never said a word. Nobody did. He just kept his eyes on his feet. I looked over at Beatrix, as I wanted to say something about the cruelty I had just witnessed.

Mary-Lynn shouted out, 'Pay attention to your own business, Maggie.'

I quickly turned my head back to Sam. He glanced up at me. He drank some more, then handed me the empty cup. I felt our fingers accidentally brush against each other's. The touch released one hundred butterflies into my stomach.

'Thank you, Maggie,' he said softly, gazing up at me.

I stepped back as he stood up. I could see Beatrix out of the corner of my eye. She was about to walk away from her husband. It was time to leave.

'I'll see you again soon,' I whispered to Sam.

He glanced over my shoulder, then looked into my eyes and gave a slight smile.

I wanted to give him a quick peck on the cheek before I left. I was Eliza. I was that woman. It was starting to get on my nerves. I wanted to be in control of my emotions. I wanted my power back. I had to stop crushing on my husband.

Mary-Lynn blew her stupid whistle again, and Sam turned away from me and walked back into the field.

I looked down glumly at the cup in my hands and wondered how I was going to stop my feelings towards this stranger.

* * *

The air in the hut was even hotter than the night before. We took turns in the shower, then ate some cold pasta dish that Sam made. We read some more of the rules, and then we took the chairs outside our front door to sit down and try to find some fresher air. Beatrix had told me that Sam had to work hard for two weeks before we could apply for a fan. She also told me not to get too excited about it because all they did was blow around warm air.

Sam sat next to me. He was quiet. Everything around us was quiet. The smell of the trees filled the air. I looked up and stargazed. The sky looked magical.

Sam pointed out a bright star in the sky and started to tell me everything he knew about astronomy. It turned out, it wasn't a lot, but what he did know impressed me.

I turned my head when I saw him shift in his seat and wince.

'What's wrong, Sam?'

He started to roll his shoulder around. 'Think I hurt my shoulder a bit today.'

'Do you need to go to the Ward?'

'No need. Just got to get used to working in the field.'

I wanted to offer to rub his shoulder, but I knew it was forbidden, and I knew he wouldn't let me.

I looked back at the stars.

All was quiet again.

I decided that we would sit like this again. I would suggest it some nights. It felt nice.

'How are you feeling, Maggie?'

I jumped slightly when he spoke. I was so lost in the peace. I was also surprised that he was making small talk, or perhaps he was just wondering if I had any aches and pains from my day.

‘I’m okay,’ I replied. I was. I felt fine. I just felt like being quiet. It had been a weird day.

There were a few more seconds of silence.

‘Do you want to go to bed?’ he asked softly.

I didn’t. I wanted to stay sitting under the stars all night, but I guessed he was probably tired and needed to sleep.

I turned to him and nodded.

We stood up, and he grabbed the chairs and brought them inside. I closed the door and turned the key.

Sam tucked the chairs back under the table, and we made our way into the bedroom. I went into the bathroom first, and then he walked in as I left.

I waited by the bed.

Sam was taking a while, so I sat down on the bed and twiddled with the small alarm clock. It was old, rusty, and had an annoyingly loud tick. I lifted my head when I heard the shower go on, and then I thought I heard him sob.

I quickly made my way over to the bathroom door. I put my ear up against it and closed my eyes.

I heard it again. I heard him crying. I wasn’t sure what to do at first.

I slowly opened the door. ‘Sam, are you all right?’

There he was, sitting in the base of the shower. He was clutching his knees into his chest. He was crying and struggling to breathe properly.

I hurried over to the shower, stepped inside, and got soaked turning it off. I quickly sat down and pulled him into my arms.

‘It’s all right,’ I said softly. ‘You’re okay. Everything’s going to be all right.’

Those were the words and actions I used whenever my big sister cried. Sometimes our mum would be too much even for her. There were times when she couldn’t breathe properly due to the tears. Later on, my sister would pretend it never happened.

Sam's arms quickly wrapped around me. He held on tightly and continued to cry.

We sat there like that for a while. I didn't know what else to do, but I did know what it felt like to break down and have nobody there to help you. So, I stayed with him until his breathing started to settle and he stopped crying.

I moved first. I gently sat back and waited for him to lift his face. I felt a trickle of water slide off the ends of my hair and make its way down my back.

'I'm sorry, Maggie.' His voice was as tired and sore as his eyes.

He had no need to be sorry. We all cry from time to time. I just wanted to know what had happened.

'What's wrong, Sam?'

He took a breath. 'This hasn't happened to me in a long while.' He stared at his trembling hands. 'I used to have panic attacks before, but they stopped when I joined Mindforder.'

He looked embarrassed.

I didn't know what to say to him.

He dropped his head into his hands. 'I'm so sorry, Maggie.' His voice breaking broke my heart.

'You have nothing to be sorry about, Sam.'

'I'm weak, Maggie.'

'No. No, you're not. You're not weak, Sam. Why would you say that about yourself? You're not weak at all.'

He shook his head in his hands and sniffed. He wouldn't look up at me. 'I've let you down.'

'No, Sam, you haven't.'

I didn't care about any repercussions. I leaned forward and held him once again. He clutched on to me. I could feel shivering, and I wasn't sure if it was me or him.

'It's gonna be all right, Sam. There's just a lot of pressure right now for us to get everything right.'

I felt his arms loosen around me. His breathing was settling down.

After a few seconds, he released himself from our hold. He looked into my eyes. He looked sad and alone.

I just felt so helpless. I had to do something.

'We're going to slow this down,' I said softly.

He took a shaky breath. 'What do you mean?'

'We're going to release some of this pressure,' I said. 'We're going to break the rules, but it'll be temporary. Just a couple of weeks. No one will know, and it will just be at home. We'll wean ourselves into this. Right now, we're no good to the Island. So, we'll let things go around here for a while, just while we get used to everything, and each other.'

He looked unsure. 'I don't know, Maggie. You shouldn't have to put yourself in a position where you could end up in trouble just because of me.'

'Let me worry about that.'

He shook his head. His eyes started to regain some warmth. 'It's my worry.'

'No one will know.' I really hoped that no one would know. I knew I was taking a major chance on him. I felt vulnerable, and I think it showed in my face.

He looked down at my hand and gently held it in his. He smiled softly, then looked back up at my insecurities.

'You're all wet, Maggie.'

I gazed over at my damp shoulder.

'Come on,' he said, shifting his body. 'Let's get you dried off.'

We stood up together in the small confinement of the shower. I could see he was a bit wobbly, probably from the tidal wave of adrenaline that had hit his body.

'Are you all right, Sam?'

He forced a fake smile as he said, 'I've seen better days.'

I wanted to hold him again.

He stood in front of me, not moving. I wasn't sure if he wanted to move, or if he couldn't because he had jelly legs, or if he was just waiting for me to move first.

I could feel a pull of energy towards him.

He moved first. He stepped outside the shower and grabbed a towel. He placed it around my shoulders as I stepped out. The caring gesture made me smile. He was wetter than me, and he only had his shorts on. I was still fully clothed and really felt like snuggling up in a pair of pyjamas.

He slowly started to take my damp dress off. He lowered the towel so that it went underneath my arms and wrapped around my body. With almost every movement he made, his hand brushed against my skin. I just stood there until all I was wearing was the white towel.

He hung up my dress on the back of the bathroom door, then placed the rest of my clothes in the white wooden laundry bin.

I handed him a towel. He wrapped it around his waist, then took off his shorts. He grabbed a hand towel and reached over and gently rubbed the tips of my hair. His soft touch was so caring. I closed my eyes for a second and embraced the warmth I felt fill me. Nobody had ever been so tender towards me. He stepped away and roughly rubbed the same towel over his own hair.

I slowly lifted my head to look over at the bedroom.

'We can lie down on the bed like this,' I said, more in a way of a suggestion.

He nodded. 'Okay.'

I went first. He followed me to the bed. We both leant over and pulled the top cover off. We quietly sat down on our allocated sides, then leaned back until our heads reached the pillows. We stared up at the ceiling. I could feel his body still trembling slightly, or maybe it was me.

'Little things like this will help lower the stress levels,' I whispered, turning to face him. 'I'll help with cooking, and we can wear tee-shirts to bed. We'll get to know stuff about each other, and it's important that we talk if we feel stressed about anything. It'll be okay if we do this.'

He turned his head to face me. His eyes smiled softly into mine. 'Just for a while.'

I smiled. 'Just for a while.'

We both turned back to face the ceiling.

'Thank you, Maggie.'

I took a slow and steady breath, one I hoped he couldn't feel. I closed my eyes.

9

Mackenzie

I was setting the tables for lunch, walking back and forth from the kitchen to the dining room. I was the only one in there. I had previously made sandwiches for everyone, guests and staff, and was told to put them out on large plates on a long table that was along one side of the room.

The other tables in the dining area were round and small. The chairs were one a table, and they faced the floor-to-ceiling windows, overlooking the side garden.

The side garden was filled with an array of withering wild flowers and pathed footpaths that seemed to go on forever.

It was quite a pleasant day outside. Mild, with a dash of sun.

The room felt warm, and I did too.

I placed the sandwiches on the table, along with some cupcakes I found on the side. Not sure who brought those in, but they looked good. They had lemon buttercream on top, with an added fondant flower, which looked pretty. I poured apple juice and orange juice into two separate jugs, and then I put out some cold-water bottles. I sat down at one of the tables and started to fold peach napkins into swans. It was my party trick. I learnt how to do it late one night via a YouTube video when I wasn't feeling very well, or more to the point, I was drunk. For some reason, my origami skills had stayed with me.

I didn't see him at first. He made me jump slightly, as he seemed to appear from nowhere.

Sam quietly sat at the table between mine and the window. He faced away from me and didn't acknowledge my existence.

I stopped what I was doing and stared at the back of his dark hair for a while. I could feel the cold atmosphere that he had brought into the room. I actually thought he was quite rude not saying hello, or anything, for that matter.

I didn't feel the need to point out his rudeness because I had spent the morning getting to know some things about him, and I knew he hadn't had the best time of it. Maybe it was for the best if we both just sat there in silence.

I carried on making my swans, but then I wondered if he was waiting on me to serve him. Victoria never said I had to serve anyone, apart from when I was doing tea rounds with the trolley.

I glanced over at the table filled with food. I hadn't put any crisps out yet, and George loved his crisps. I looked over at the large white clock on the wall behind me. There was nearly fifteen minutes till lunch. Sam was early.

'You can eat now if you like,' I called over to him, whilst adjusting a swan.

I saw his head shift slightly, out of the top of my eyes.

He remained silent.

So far, I had made three swans. I got up and placed one down on the table in front of him, next to the cutlery. I thought it might cheer him up.

I sat back down and started to make another swan.

There was silence for a while, then he spoke.

'What's that supposed to be, a dinosaur?'

His Irish accent was soft, but his tone was hostile. He wasn't making friends with me.

'It's a swan,' I said flatly. I watched the back of him to see if he moved at all.

He did. He looked over his shoulder at me. He had a nice face, even with the fed-up look that was washed all over it. He wasn't giving off any warmth, and yet, there was something about his eyes that held kindness. I could see it. I could feel his energy. It wasn't matching his persona.

My parents had always told me that I had a gift of picking up on other people's emotions. It wasn't a gift to me. I had learned a long time ago how to shut that down. Feeling other people's pain wasn't in my best interest. In fact, it was quite draining at times. I had to teach myself how to disconnect.

The disconnection was failing me. I connected with Sam the moment I looked into his eyes. I wasn't sure if he connected back. He did pause when he saw me. He blinked a couple of times. He might have been pondering over his next set of words, or maybe he had no words.

While he was still looking at me, he reached back and removed the swan from the table and flicked it out to his side. Then, he placed the unfolded napkin back down on his table.

I thought about my six-year-old cousin, Kirsty. That's exactly the type of defiant thing she would have done if she hadn't got her own way about something.

I wondered if he was testing my patience. George did say Sam wasn't a fan of people. He knew I was a newbie at Moreton Hall. Maybe he was trying to get me to react so that I would get fired.

Challenge accepted.

I slowly got up and walked over to him. I placed another swan down on his table. As my arm lifted, I caught a small flinch in his eye. It concerned me. Did he think I was going to hit him?

He watched me until I sat back down, and then he turned his back on me again.

I sighed to myself and was about to make another swan when he swiped his swan off his table, using his arm in one big agitated swoop.

It made me jump. I swore under my breath. I wondered what he was going to do next. I wondered what I should do next.

He shot up out of his chair, which made me do the same. He didn't move, neither did I.

I had to say something. I had great customer service skills from working in a pub. I knew how to calm down rowdy people.

'Are you okay, Sam?' I asked softly.

His head lowered. He didn't answer.

I tried to make friends. 'My name's Mackenzie, but everyone calls me Mac.'

Still nothing.

I went over to him and leaned down to pick up the napkin.

His hand shot out to the side. 'Leave it alone,' he snapped. 'I'll do it,' he added, his voice softening.

I straightened up and took a step back.

He bent down and grabbed the napkin and placed it back onto the table. Not once did he look at me.

'I'm sorry, Mackenzie,' he said quietly. 'Now, would you let me be to eat my lunch, please.'

He wasn't really asking. He was politely telling me to go away.

'Yes,' I whispered.

I walked into the kitchen to fetch the crisps. Sam was putting food on his plate when I returned. I placed a bowl on the table and filled it with a large bag of ready salted.

We stood next to each other as he poured himself some orange juice. I didn't want to pick anything up because I was feeling awkward, which meant I would get clumsy. I stood there staring at the egg and cress sandwiches until he turned to walk away.

He stopped, paused, and then looked over his shoulder. ‘Make sure you eat something, Mackenzie. Every day in here is a long one.’

I looked directly at him.

He nodded towards the food.

I gave a slight nod back.

He didn’t move. He just nodded at the sandwiches again. It appeared he wanted me to eat one there and then. It didn’t look as though he were going to move until I picked one up, so I did.

He raised his eyebrows at me.

I bit into one corner of the triangle, while looking in his eyes.

He turned back to his table.

I was sure he smiled.

10

When most people want to talk to their friends they call or text them. That wasn't the road I went down when I wanted to talk to Adam.

I had once bought a large bag of gravel from the local pet shop. It was light grey and in need of a florescent light, some aquatic plants, and a couple of goldfish to go with it.

I was not the owner of a fish tank. I was the owner of a bag of gravel that was for splattering against Adam's window to gain his attention.

I grabbed a small handful and threw it over with such force that if it had been the little rock type of gravel, it would have chipped the glass.

Adam's venetian blind was tightly closed.

I waited for the slats to move.

There was still no movement after twenty seconds, and I really wasn't about to wait any longer. I grabbed another handful. It hit the pane at the same time that he raised his blind all the way up to the top of the window.

The gravel clearly made him jump. He glared at the glass, then over at me.

I stared blankly. I had no regrets. We both knew I lacked patience.

He slid his window up.

I could only see the top half of him. He was wearing a navy-blue tee-shirt that had Pink Floyd scribbled in white across the middle.

I spoke before he had a chance to say whatever his stern expression was itching to release.

‘What’s wrong, Adds? You haven’t been swimming.’

He knew better than to come back with a gameplay of *what do you mean* or something equally a waste of time.

‘I had a row with my mum,’ he said.

Adam and Malorie hardly ever argued. They had a great relationship, so I knew it had to be over something major.

‘And that’s stopped you from swimming?’ I asked flatly.

I sensed he was sulking.

His face tightened.

‘Do you want to talk about it?’ I added.

He shrugged. ‘It was over me wanting to move out.’

I was a bit surprised. He’d never mentioned anything about moving out to me.

‘Why do you want to move out?’ I asked, after clearing a lump that had formed in the back of my throat.

‘I’m just ready to live on my own,’ he said simply. ‘No big deal. I’m older, and I just want my own place.’

‘You’re there most of the time on your own as it is. It’s practically your place,’ I said, pointing at his house.

‘It’s not the same.’

‘So, you’re not going to swim until she agrees?’ I questioned.

The corners of his mouth curled to reveal his full-on cute smile. ‘Yeah, I guess I went into brat mode, didn’t I?’

I nodded. ‘How are you feeling?’

‘Stupid,’ he replied.

‘I meant, how is your body feeling from not swimming for two weeks?’

‘Oh, not bad, actually.’ He seemed surprised.

‘Why don’t you go for a swim now,’ I suggested.

He quickly said, ‘Only if you come and talk to me while I do my laps.’

That was a first. He must have been feeling worse than he was letting on.

'Will you even hear me while you're swimming?' I asked.

His eyes smiled over at me. 'I'll try.'

I glanced down at my lap. 'I'm in my pyjamas.'

'I can see that.'

I shrugged. 'Okay, I'll be there in a minute.'

He grinned. 'I'll leave the side gate unlocked.'

* * *

The humidity of the enclosed pool area hit me straight away. I had my hair tied up in a messy bun on top of my head, but I knew instantly that it had frizzed into extra mess. I knew it would happen. There was no escape.

I also knew it would be muggy in there, so I had swapped my long pyjama bottoms for matching short ones. It was a pink flowery set that George had bought me for my last birthday. It came with a matching eye mask and slippers.

I brought a cup of tea with me, as I figured I might need some company while Adam did his laps. My 'I love cats' mug was my evening's choice.

When I saw that Adam was already swimming in the pool, I knew he had already made the decision to go for a swim before my suggestion. There was no way he would have beat me to the pool otherwise, even with the lift in his house and the pit stop I made to my kitchen.

Adam's mum had pondered over the idea of moving when he first had his accident, but decided to renovate their home instead. She had enough money to live in a huge house, but she once told me that two people taking up that much space while a lot of people in our country lived in overcrowded conditions was just ridiculous.

Adam's home was filled with a lot of fancy gadgets that made his life easier. Even his wheelchair was designed by some woman who worked as an engineer for NASA. She was one of Malorie's friends who had offered her help after the car crash. Adam always had a lot of help in his life. Malorie had always showered him with love, but she was fiercely independent and had raised her son to be the same.

I sat down at the edge of the pool and dangled my legs into the tepid water. I immediately felt relaxed. I glanced down to see if I was at the deep end or the shallow end, but I quickly noticed that the rectangular pool was the same depth throughout.

I remembered when it was built. Malorie had told my mum that the pool was for Adam's exercises only. There wasn't going to be any pool parties, pool guests, inflatable lilos, volleyball games, or any playtime whatsoever. She pretty much told the whole street before anyone had the chance to ask for a quick dip.

I watched Adam swimming towards me and wondered if he had only invited me into his restricted domain just to be even more of a brat to his mum.

He came to a stop beside me and rested his arms on the side. His sky-blue eyes sparkled up at me. 'Did you make me tea?' he asked, nodding towards my cup.

'You can have tea when you're finished,' I told him. 'How many laps have you done so far?'

'Four.'

I pointed down the other end of the pool. 'Off you go then.'

He grinned.

I smiled back. I couldn't help myself. He had one of those smiles that made you always want to smile back.

‘Tell me about your day in your new job as I swim,’ he said.

I tried to stay focused on his eyes. My eyes wanted to roll down to admire his upper body strength.

I told myself to stop it. It’s Adam.

‘Okay,’ I said. ‘I’ll talk, you swim.’

He turned away and went into a front crawl.

I started to talk about everything I was allowed to say about Moreton Hall, which wasn’t much. Not that it mattered. I knew Adam couldn’t hear me. I had a little moan about a few things and scoffed about a few other things. I rambled away to myself and cleared everything from my mind that was weird about my day.

I felt better afterwards. I realised that I could do with swimming pool therapy more often.

Adam pulled himself out of the water to sit by my side. He wiped his wet finger down my nose and laughed as I wriggled my face away.

We both looked down at our legs dangling in the water. I knew I was the only one who could feel the sensation of the liquid. A wave of sadness hit me.

I leant my head down onto his damp shoulder. I felt his head rest on top of mine.

‘I don’t want you to move away, Adds,’ I said quietly.

He reached over and held my hand. His thumb gently stroked my skin. ‘We all grow up and move on one day, Mac.’

My stupid lip trembled against my will. ‘I’ll miss you.’

He gently squeezed my hand. ‘Come on, Mac. You know I’ll never be far away from you.’

I didn’t know. All I knew was everything was starting to change, and I didn’t like how it felt. It was a similar feeling to what I had when George went away to uni. It was strange not having him in my life 24/7. The thought of Adam leaving was even worse. What would I do without him in his window advising me, putting me straight, sticking up pictures and poems to cheer me up?

Growing up wasn't as much fun as I thought it was going to be. No one told me you can lose everyone you love. I didn't want to lose Adam. Not him.

He raised my hand and kissed it gently. 'It'll be all right, you'll see,' he said softly, as though reading my mind.

We sat for a while in silence, holding on to our friendship for as long as possible.

I felt him lift his head.

I turned to look into his wondering eyes.

'Who's Sam?' he asked.

11

Victoria had told me to write down anything that I witnessed Sam say or do. I felt like a spy for the next few days until Claire told me it was okay.

I was sitting in her room, I guess you could say, making friends. She was due to leave soon, but she still took the time to get to know me. She was sweet and friendly, softly spoken, and had a humbleness about her.

‘You just have to treat guests in here the same way you would treat anyone,’ she told me.

‘But George told me to be gentle.’

Claire shrugged. ‘We’re just people.’

‘Traumatised people,’ I added quickly.

She nodded. ‘True, but it’s still nice when you’re treated the same as everyone else.’

‘How were you treated in your cult?’

She lowered her head slightly and smiled sweetly at her hands. ‘I like the way you just come right out and say the word cult. It’s not widely used around here, strangely enough.’

I rarely stopped to think. I didn’t have one of those edit filters. ‘Sorry, too cold?’ I asked.

She looked at me. ‘No, just right. It is what it is, at the end of the day. No point sugar-coating it. I wasn’t treated very well, Mac. It’s not a good place, especially if you’re a woman.’

‘Why didn’t you just leave once you realised it was a bad place?’

She looked out the window and paused before replying.

‘You don’t see it at first, then when you do, you let things go because they seem small, or you get an apology. You want to be there. You feel like family. You don’t want to be thrown out. After a while, you’re conditioned. You don’t even see it happening to you. It’s the dripping tap effect.’

‘Dripping tap effect?’ I asked.

She nodded and sat down on the corner of her bed, opposite me. ‘Drip, drip, drip. You don’t realise until your sink is overflowing. By then, it’s too late.’

‘Do you think you’d still be there today if your parents didn’t get you out?’

She shook her head slightly. ‘I really don’t know.’

I couldn’t begin to understand what her life had been like living in a cult, or what it was like before that. ‘What made you join in the first place?’

A warmth filled her face. ‘I felt like I belonged somewhere.’

I kind of knew how she felt. I didn’t feel I belonged anywhere much. I felt my life lacked purpose, and I didn’t hold out much hope for my future.

‘I don’t think I’m the type who would join a cult,’ I told her, without thinking how that might sound.

The corners of her mouth curled. ‘We’re all looking for somewhere to call home, Mac.’

I glanced over at the tea trolley waiting for me outside her bedroom door. ‘I feel at home in my own home. I just don’t know where else I fit.’

‘You’ll figure it out. Sometimes it takes time.’

‘How long did it take for you to figure out you’re better off now?’

She thought about it. It wasn’t something she knew straight away. ‘I’m thinking I was here just over a year when

I started to change.' She looked me straight in the eyes. 'I had a lot of healing to do before I could get my head straight.'

'I would have thought it would come hand in hand.'

She shook her head. 'I guess everyone's different, but mostly, you need to heal before you can move forward.'

We sat in silence for a minute. I wasn't sure if she was reflecting, or perhaps just waiting on her cup of tea that I still hadn't poured.

'What will you do now?' I asked.

'Go home. Spend some time adjusting to that home. I haven't really got past that part yet.'

'One step at a time.'

She smiled. 'It's always the best way.'

I got up to make her a cup of tea. 'Are you surprised you have been here so long?'

'Not really. I have a lot of patience. It takes as long as it takes.'

I thought about my own patience. Never really had any. I dropped a teabag inside a mug and flipped the switch on the small urn. I watched the hot water flow out. I waited a few seconds for the tea to brew.

'I don't take milk,' she called out to me.

I removed the teabag and brought the cup to her. 'I've never had a cuppa without milk before. I even poured it into a cup of Earl Grey once. My dad called me a philistine.'

She laughed. 'I hate milk.'

I sat on her bed, opposite her.

Claire blew into her cup, then rolled her eyes up at me. 'What about you, Mac? What do you want to do with your life?'

'Oh, you've got me now, Claire,' I scoffed. 'I haven't got a bloody clue. I would have thought that was obvious.'

'Why would that be obvious?'

‘Because I’m pushing around a tea trolley.’

She kind of scolded me with her sweet eyes. ‘Some people are very happy to push around a tea trolley. They choose to do that.’

I shrugged. I wasn’t trying to put down all the tea trolley pushers in the world.

‘I guess what I’m really trying to say is that I’ve hit a dead end with my life.’

‘How old are you, Mac?’

‘Twenty-three.’

‘My father would tell you that you have the world at your feet at that age.’

‘The world might be at my feet, but that doesn’t mean I know what to do with it.’

She giggled and attempted to sip her hot tea.

‘I don’t know why we’re expected to know what to do with our lives as soon as we leave school anyway,’ I said.

‘My father wants me to study something.’

I scoffed. ‘Mine’s just happy I’ve got another job. I’ve kept my first job. I just cut my hours. I work a couple of evenings a week in a pub near where I live.’

‘Would you like to go back to school, Mac? Study something? Do you have any interests?’

She started to sound like George. The questions triggered my brain into thinking about what did interest me. I wasn’t really coming up with anything, which made for a long pause.

Claire smiled softly. ‘It doesn’t matter. One day, you’ll find your dream.’

I frowned. ‘Do people find their dreams? I thought it was something you either had or you didn’t have.’

‘Sometimes dreams come to you when you least expect them.’

Claire sounded so much wiser than me. She seemed so ready for the outside world. She would do well in a job like George's. She was comfortable to be around. She was a good listener, and she didn't push her opinions on you. I liked her energy. I selfishly wished she was going to stay longer. She had warmth in her, and it shone through her every pore. She really was nice company.

'Maybe I'll find a subject I'd like to study, one day,' I said quietly.

'You can always come and visit me for a holiday. Perhaps something in my life might trigger a dream for you.'

'Aw, that's a nice thing to say, Claire. Where do you live?'

'Cotswolds, but I think my dad wants to take me to Iceland for a while. We have a home there as well because he travels there a lot through work. My mum wants me to go to our farm in Australia, but Dad's never keen. He hates the heat.' She giggled to herself. 'You would think he would be used to it. He's from Jamaica.'

'Why did your parents buy a place in Australia?'

'My mum's Australian. They met in New York, through work. I was born here, my eldest brother was born in America, and my youngest brother was born in Iceland.'

'Wow, your family like to get around.'

Claire drank some tea, then placed her cup on the floor by her feet. 'Don't you want to travel?'

'I guess it would be nice, but I would have to save up a lot first.'

'I'm not sure I want to travel.' She looked deep in thought. 'I do miss the horses on the farm, but it's been so long now.' She looked over at me. 'The last six months have been all about me getting reacquainted with my family, so that I feel comfortable in that circle again.'

‘How did it go, or how is it still going?’

She nodded. ‘Yeah, good. My mum couldn’t stop crying the first time she saw me here. She still has the odd sniffle. My brothers were great, and Dad was just Dad.’

‘Do you have a nice family then?’

‘Yes, I am blessed in that area of my life.’

I was thinking she was blessed in many areas of her life. She was pretty, smart, caring, rich, and loved.

She grinned at me. ‘I know what you’re thinking, Mac. You’re wondering why someone like me, with a happy, rich family would feel lost enough to run away to live with a cult.’

I shrugged. ‘Not going to lie, Claire. It did run through my mind.’

‘It’s simple, really. Neither money nor other people’s love can make you happy. Happiness is an inside job. You have to find it within you. You have to feel at peace with yourself. You have to feel at home with yourself.’

I was about to tell her that she was wise beyond her years and that she was completely right, when Victoria appeared in the doorway.

‘Claire, your father will be here shortly. Do you want to come downstairs now?’

We both looked at Victoria.

‘Sure,’ said Claire. She bent over to retrieve her cup. She gulped down the remaining tea, as though leaving some behind would offend me, and then handed me the empty mug.

Victoria said to me, ‘Sam is in the garden. Why don’t you take him out a cup of tea, Mackenzie.’

It wasn’t a suggestion. It also wasn’t something I was keen to do, but I got on with it.

* * *

Sam was sitting on a wooden bench, staring out at the lake. The sun was going down, and a chill was starting to fill the air. I was slightly worried the hot mug of tea I was holding would go cold before I got to him. I didn't want to give him something to moan about.

He shifted in his seat as I approached. Not sure if he had heard me or sensed my presence.

I sat down at the other end of the bench and offered him the drink.

He glanced sideways at the cup. 'No,' he said flatly.

I took a mouthful. It burned my tongue. That metal urn did a good job at keeping the water boiling hot. I placed the tea down on the wooden slats between us, but my hand wobbled and the cup tipped sideways. I made a quick grab for it before the whole lot reached his bottoms, but it was too late. Hot tea had scolded the side of his leg.

Sam yelped and swore under his breath as he jumped away to the far end of the bench.

I quickly took charge of the cup. 'Oh my God! I'm so sorry.'

His chest rose steadily, and a controlled breath left his nose.

I tried to flick away the remnants of tea left on the seat. Some of it spat onto him.

His face shot my way. 'What the… I swear to…' He didn't finish his sentence.

'Sorry,' I mumbled. I bit my lip inwards so that I didn't laugh. I stopped fidgeting and stared forward.

The garden was nice, and the air smelled of fresh linen. The lake made me feel peaceful, and I found myself no longer caring what Sam might think or say next. I didn't even care if he upped and left. I had already decided I was going to stay awhile, even though I did feel a tad cold.

Sam had more sense than me. He had brought out a fleece jacket with him. I realised that the fresh linen smell was coming from that. He looked cosy and warm in the early evening.

I, on the other hand, had cropped dark jeans and a thin, long-sleeved top. It was my favourite one because it simply draped on me and never caused me to constantly make body adjustments. I liked clothes that didn't make me fidget. Clothes that I could breathe freely in. I also liked colours, which my bright yellow top pretty much told the world.

I shivered. 'Are you cold?' I asked.

His head turned sharply. 'What, after having boiling hot tea spilled on me?'

It was obvious he was still a tad angry about that.

Sam glanced down at the cup, then back at the lake. He crossed his ankles and turned slightly away from me.

I chewed on the inside of my gum to stop myself from saying anything else.

We sat in silence for a few minutes. Seemed like forever. When he spoke, I jumped.

'What are you doing here?' he asked, as though the question had been simmering in his mind, annoying him.

'I brought you tea.'

He still wasn't looking at me.

'I mean here, Moreton Hall.'

'I got a job.'

Silence for another minute. Then, I felt a bit smart.

'What are you doing here?' I asked.

'I find the lake peaceful,' he replied flatly.

'I mean here, Moreton Hall,' I said quickly, before my brain had time to tell me that George would not approve of the question.

'I joined a cult,' he replied, just as quickly.

Now I sounded stupid, and I knew that we both knew that.

More silence.

I remembered Claire telling me that I should treat the guests the same way I would anyone. So, I asked the question that was on my mind.

'Who's Maggie?'

Not too sure at that point whether something inside of him had just silently exploded, or if he was contemplating answering my intrusive question. Perhaps he was thinking about her. Whatever he was thinking, it made his body tighten as much as his face.

There was a long silence. There was no way I was going to ask again. I could feel his emotions stirring. I could feel his energy shift. I had already burned his leg, and now I'd touched a nerve. I had the feeling if I did anything else it was quite possible he would shot put me into the lake.

'My best friend,' he said softly.

I wasn't expecting him to say anything. I felt I had to continue the conversation.

'Do you want to talk about her?' I asked.

His face softened a touch. 'What do you want to know?'

'I don't want to know anything in particular,' I lied. 'I read some of your file. Not because I was being nosy.' I felt the need to clarify. 'We have to know about the guests.'

'I know,' he said gently.

I loved how soft his accent was, when he wasn't snapping at me. 'I read that you tried to kill yourself when you got here, and George said it was because of Maggie.'

He huffed out a laugh and shook his head slightly as his eyes turned to his knees. 'You just come right out and say what you're thinking, don't you?'

I allowed my empathy to enter my eyes as he turned to me. I tried not to shiver as a cold breeze went straight through my clothes. 'What did she do to you?'

He stared at me for a moment, and then he unzipped his jacket, took it off, leaned towards me, and carefully wrapped it around my shoulders.

The unexpected kind gesture warmed me more than his fleece. 'Thank you, but you didn't have to.'

He removed his eyes from my face to look down at his lap.

I kept my eyes on him. 'What did she do to you, Sam?' I asked softly.

His eyelids flickered. 'She loved me.'

I pulled the jacket around me, snuggling deeper into his kindness. 'Oh, I thought she might have been one of your abusers at Mindforder.'

His head moved slightly towards me. 'No. That wasn't her.'

12

Maggie

We were sitting on the bed eating peanut butter on toast and drinking cold milk. We knew we had to make the most of it because our two-week time-out was about to come to an end as of tomorrow.

Sam was smiling at me. 'You've got peanut butter on your cheek.'

I wiped it away and smiled back. 'How is it possible that you didn't leave any crumbs behind?' I glanced down at the blue tee-shirt I was wearing that belonged to him. 'I've got crumbs everywhere.'

'It might have something to do with the fact that I put my hand under my mouth when I ate mine. Have you thought about trying that manoeuvre out, Maggie?'

I watched him stretch his arms up in the air before reaching down for his cup on the floor. 'We can't all be as neat and tidy as you.'

He laughed. 'I noticed.'

His matching tee-shirt was clean and less creased than mine.

We wore his tee-shirts a lot indoors. I did have a house dress. It was like a three-quarter length slip. It had spaghetti straps and was made from a thin beige material. I wasn't allowed to wear it outside. It was strictly for home use only. It was the coolest item of clothing I had. My outdoor dresses were too thick for the heat, but whoever designed them didn't seem to care. Sam's tee-shirts were a blessing. We had to clean them inside and hang them in the bathroom. We didn't want anyone to notice that Sam was going through a lot of tops over the last two weeks.

'Back to normal tomorrow, Maggie.'

My shoulders drooped. I had really enjoyed our two weeks. Each day that had passed by seemed like a week. It felt relaxed and normal at home, and we had become good friends. I loved every minute I spent in his company. I couldn't wait to leave my chores and get home to him each night. We had laughed in the kitchen when he tried to teach me how to cook, and we had talked in bed every night way into the early hours of the morning.

He had told me some of his backstory. He was born in London to an English dad and an Irish mum. His dad died when he was four, and his mum took him from London to live in Ireland, somewhere not far from Dublin. He joined Mindforder when he was seventeen, after his friend had introduced him to a local group in the city, and he went off to live in the Leicester village.

I didn't say too much about my own past, just that I had a mum and sister, and we were from East London, and that I lived in the Somerset village when I joined Mindforder.

Sam was relaxed, smiling loads, and warm and friendly towards me. He even let me make him a cup of tea. Everything felt nice. I didn't want to mention my past and bring doom and gloom into our home.

He removed the plate filled with crumbs and placed it on the floor on his side of the bed. I put my milk down on the floor on my side. It had gone warm, and I was already feeling the night-time heat creep up on me.

I leant forward and folded the sheets over so that they were at the bottom of the bed, and then I flopped backwards onto my cool pillow, which didn't stay cool for long.

Sam joined me.

We both had our arms down at our sides. The sides of our hands were touching, but neither of us moved.

'No more tee-shirts tomorrow,' he said.

I turned my head to face him. 'I don't mind if we keep that part.'

He looked at me with raised eyebrows. 'We agreed, two weeks only.'

'Okay,' I said quietly.

'We have a job here, Maggie. It's what we signed up for. We've helped ourselves so that we can be at the top of our game to help the Island.'

I didn't speak.

'Think of the babies,' he added.

'Okay,' I said again, trying not to smile.

He took a deep breath, and then, much to my surprise, he held my hand.

The sensation of happiness rushed through me. I looked into his gentle eyes as he looked into mine.

He turned away first. He looked up at the ceiling.

I glanced over at the clock. I told myself not to say anything but went ahead and said it anyway. 'Sam, will you do one last thing for me before it turns midnight and we go back to normal?'

I turned to see the corners of his mouth curl up. 'What do you want me to do, Cinderella?'

'Will you kiss me? Just once.'

I didn't care what his answer would be, or the fact that I could be deported. I was too busy admiring myself for having the guts to ask. Being wrapped up in myself didn't last long because he turned to face me.

Sam let go of my hand and slowly leaned up so that he was resting on his elbow. He looked down into my eyes. I could feel my heart beating. He lowered his face towards me and placed his lips on mine. They felt soft and warm. His hand came up and gently touched my face. The kiss seemed to last a long time, and there weren't any fireworks going off. It didn't feel like a first kiss. It felt comfortable, like he had kissed me many times before. He then slowly pulled away, and his eyes gave me a small smile. He rested his head back down upon his pillow and looked back at the ceiling.

'Thank you,' I whispered.

'You're welcome.'

I watched his face break out into a big smile, and I had to laugh too.

He looked over at me. 'You know we can't ever do that again, right?'

I giggled. 'I know.'

He jumped up to turn off the light and just as quickly got back into bed. He turned over on his side, away from me. 'Get some sleep now.'

'Nunnight, Sam,' I whispered into the darkness of the room.

A muffled laugh came from him. 'Sleep well, Maggie.'

* * *

The next few weeks were a lot easier than the first couple of days we had spent on the Island. It did make me wonder if any of the other couples had ever tried anything like we had to relax around each other. I knew I couldn't ask anyone.

We were both on a high. We were relaxed, happy, focused, and we both felt that we were bringing strong, positive energy to the Island for the babies.

Life was good, and we were settled. Although, there was something that was still unsettling me. It was the husband who worked with Sam who hardly received any water from his wife.

I wasn't the only one who had noticed, which I found out when Sam came in from work one evening.

I could see that he was annoyed about something. His usual friendly face was tense, and his eyes lacked warmth. He practically slammed his hat down on the side by the door, and then he threw his white hand towel into the bathroom.

I stood still, watching his every agitated move. The tension unnerved me.

He went into the kitchen to set out dinner. He opened the fridge and took out his homemade potato salad. The dish banged heavily onto the table. The fact that I jumped made him realise just how heavy-handed he was being around the house.

'Sorry,' he said softly, lowering his head submissively. His eyes rolled up to look me over. 'I'm sorry, Maggie. Are you okay?'

I nodded and slipped my feet out of my shoes, and then I went into the bathroom to control my exhale and calm my nerves. I freshened up and put on my indoor dress.

Cold chicken fillets and a green salad was sitting on the table by the time I came out. Placed there a lot quieter.

I took my place at the table.

Sam brought me a jug and a glass. The jug was half filled with orange juice. His eyes were boring into my face.

'Maggie, are you okay?'

'I am,' I replied, avoiding his eyes.

'You can be jumpy, Maggie,' he said softly. 'Sometimes I worry about that.'

I was staring down at my lap, twiddling my fingers. 'I just don't like tension,' I said quietly. 'Or anger,' I decided to add.

He bowed slightly. 'I'll not bring that to your life again. I don't want you to ever be scared of me.'

'You don't scare me, Sam. It's just…' I didn't want to finish my sentence.

He finished it for me. 'Somebody once did.'

I steadied my breathing. 'It's okay.'

'No. It's not,' he said gently.

Neither of us moved for a few seconds.

I raised my eyes to meet his. All I could see was concern.

'Are you all right, Maggie?'

'I am, but you're not,' I said quietly. 'Do you want to talk about it?'

His chest heaved a deep sigh. He turned away to grab some cutlery from the drawer, and then he sat down opposite me.

I waited for him to hand me a knife and fork, and then I asked my question again.

'I'm okay,' he said gently.

We both knew that wasn't true.

I didn't eat anything on my plate.

He had already swallowed a mouthful of chicken before he realised I hadn't touched my food.

He nodded towards the table. 'Eat your dinner, Maggie.'

'No,' I said, not meaning for my tone to sound so stubborn.

He put down his fork and sipped his juice while staring over at me.

I tried to keep my expression neutral. 'I'm not eating tonight.'

'Why not?'

My forehead tightened. 'You know why.'

He slowly put his glass down. 'Because of my attitude?'

I folded my arms. 'No, Sam. Because you won't tell me what's upset you.'

He placed his hands on his lap. 'I won't be able to eat, if you don't eat. You know that.'

I remained silent.

'Maggie, please. I'm hungry. I've been working hard all day.'

Guilt rushed through me, so I took a piece of lettuce and shoved it in my mouth.

He raised his eyebrows at me. 'Really?'

'I thought we were going to talk about everything.' My words were muffled through my munched lettuce.

He picked up his knife and fork, then lowered his eyes to his plate. 'You know I can't talk about everything.'

I quickly swallowed the food in my mouth. 'You can to me,' I said softly.

He ate a lump of salad, then reluctantly said, 'I'm a bit worried about something, that's all.'

'You can talk to me about that. I might be able to help.'

He was clearly thinking it over. Finally, he said, 'It's about one of the farmers.'

I knew straight away it was about the man who got no water. It had to be.

'His name is Ross,' he added. 'He looks so ill, Maggie. Like he is not fed or watered at all.' He paused for a moment. 'His wife pours his water away right there in front of him on the field.'

I gave a slight nod. 'I've seen her do that.'

'That can't be right. Surely someone must have words with her.'

'Have you thought about telling Mary-Lynn?' I asked.

'No. I'm not sure if I'm allowed.'

I glanced over at the rule book on the side next to Sam's hat. We still hadn't mastered it.

'What should we do, Maggie?'

I turned back to him. 'I don't know if it's our place to do anything, Sam.'

'She's hurting him.'

'Maybe she's disciplining him.'

'Maggie, the man's dehydrated. He is sure to collapse one day. One day soon, that is. You cannot discipline someone to death.'

'We don't know the full story.'

'No, we don't. We just know that he is suffering. Have you seen the size of him? There's hardly anything left of the man.'

'We could get in trouble if we interfere.'

'He could die if we don't.'

We both stared down at our food.

Sam sighed. 'I'm sorry, Maggie. I know I shouldn't be talking this way, especially to you, but I'm worried for the man, you know. We're supposed to be a family. We're supposed to care about each other.'

'We do care,' I said softly.

'I don't feel like we do. Not here. It's not the same as it is in the villages. Everything feels different here.'

I knew he was right. Life on the Island was so different to life in the villages.

'We have to be more disciplined here, Sam. You know that.'

He sipped his juice, then stabbed his chicken with his fork. He stared at it for a second before putting it back down on his plate.

'The wife is being cruel, Maggie,' he said quietly. 'I feel uncomfortable about that.'

He wasn't the only one. 'Leave it with me, Sam. I'll talk to Beatrix about it. See what advice she can offer. I'll tell her I've noticed. I won't mention you.'

He gave a nod. 'Okay.'

I looked over at his plate. 'Eat your dinner now, Sam.'

He looked like he had gone right off his food. No doubt thinking about Ross and whether or not he was being fed tonight. That's what I was thinking.

'Eat, Sam,' I said softly. 'You're not to get ill.'

His eyes rolled up to look into mine.

I felt a flutter in my stomach, and it wasn't because I hadn't eaten.

He then nodded at my plate. 'After you, Maggie.'

I picked up my knife and fork and cut up some chicken and ate it, all the while looking directly into his gentle eyes.

Sam smiled and started to eat his dinner properly.

I looked down at my plate and thought about what exactly I could say to Beatrix, and how she might respond.

* * *

The words had been floating around in my head all night and all morning. I couldn't wait to get Beatrix alone to ask her about Ross and his wife.

'We can't get involved with that, Maggie,' said Beatrix. She had her eyes wide open, her mouth half gaping, and her voice was kept low. She nervously looked around us.

We were the only ones on the footpath leading up towards the Kitchen.

'Surely, it must be wrong,' I questioned.

Beatrix shrugged. 'Joanne does seem to be going a bit overboard this time, I'll admit. She often treats him this way.

Ross looks like he's one step away from the Ward at all times, but it's not our place.'

'Then, whose place is it?'

'Mary-Lynn. She's in charge over there.'

'She's not doing anything about it,' I said quickly. 'She must have seen what's going on. We have.'

Beatrix stopped walking. She grabbed my arms tightly. Her face was filled with fear. 'Maggie, if you know what's good for you, you'll let this go. You don't want to be punished for not minding your own business. Besides, she'll fatten him up again soon. It's pretty much an on and off situation with those two.'

I released myself from her grip. 'What's this punishment all about?' I asked. 'No one ever got punished in the villages. Mindforder is about the freedom of women, and bringing positivity to the world, so where in any of that does punishment fit in?'

'It's different here, Maggie. Here, you can be punished. Life has to be strict here.'

She had me worried. 'How are you punished? What happens to you? Are you just kicked off the Island?'

She pulled me back along the pathway. 'Come on, we'll be late.'

'Tell me about the punishment,' I whispered.

She shook her head. 'Just pray you never find out.'

I did a quick silent prayer that I never found out, but I did find out. I got to witness it with my own eyes. It was about a month after Beatrix had left for good.

13

There was some exciting news going around the Island. Beatrix had been invited to go and work up at the Main House. Tom had been asked to decide whether he wanted to stay on as a Guardian or go back to a village. He chose to leave.

I knew instantly how much I was going to miss Beatrix. She was my closest friend out of all the wives. She helped me learn the rules. She gave me good advice. She never once reported me for gossiping or asking awkward questions. She made me feel safe during the four months I had known her. I didn't want her to go, but I knew that it was a wonderful opportunity for her.

It wasn't very often that a wife was invited to join the Main House. I figured someone up there had decided to go back to the villages, so there was an opening.

Beatrix was so excited. It was all she could talk about for days. It was all any of us could talk about for days.

We only had two weeks to make the preparations for her departure.

Two weeks before we said our goodbyes.

There was a special assembly held, dedicated just to Beatrix. We all sat inside the hall and watched her stand at the front alongside Rochelle. I was sure her cheeks were hurting from the constant smile spread across her face.

We all got the shock of our lives when Buddy walked in and took to the stage.

I felt Sam squeeze my hand.

Buddy was dressed in simple plain clothes like the rest of us, but he stood out like a beacon. Just his presence alone lifted the room. He didn't need to say a word.

Hushed excitement filled the hall until Buddy held up his arms to quieten us.

He held Beatrix's hand, and she looked as though she had just won a million pounds.

Buddy gave a warm speech, which included many thanks for our dedication and service to our religion. He told us how important and valued we were.

I had never felt so proud of myself. Happiness filled every part of me. I was strong, needed, wanted, and I made a difference in the world.

Buddy's words were so kind and genuine. I was swept away by his depth and loyalty to us all.

We listened carefully to everything he had to say, and we all felt so privileged to have him in our lives.

Sam and I were so excited when it came to our turn to meet him.

We stood in front of him, our hands clenched tightly together. I wanted to hold Buddy's hand, to hug him, to kiss him on the cheek. I wanted him to stay talking to us forever. Everything made sense when he spoke. Everything made sense when he was around.

Buddy thanked us personally and told us to keep up the good work. He looked me directly in the eyes and smiled warmly as he said my name. He actually said my name.

I was as high as the stars, and it was the best feeling in the world. I didn't want him to leave, but it was time for him to go.

We were all ushered over to the Barn where we had a party for Beatrix, which consisted of tea, juice, sandwiches, and cakes. All of the husbands were allowed to attend, but we weren't allowed to touch or speak to each other inside there. Sam caught my eye every so often and smiled my way.

The air inside the Barn was filled with pure joy. Everyone was fully charged and in the best of spirits.

Beatrix was in her element. She was the main attraction, and rightly so.

We watched as Rochelle gifted Beatrix with a new dress fit for the Main House. It was so much prettier than ours. It was a cream summer dress made from cotton.

Beatrix flopped it over the front of her body for us all to see. She gave a twirl, and we all clapped.

The party seemed to go on forever. It ended up a long night. My feet were sore from my hard shoes, and I couldn't wait to go home with Sam so that we could talk about Buddy.

Beatrix and Tom said goodbye to us all at the end of the party, and we got to wave them away like we would at a wedding.

It was one of the happiest days I had on the Island, and one of the saddest in some ways. I hoped that one day I would see Beatrix again. I hoped that one day I might be invited to work at the Main House.

To be considered so important was such an honour. I would meet Bluebird, and she would know who I was, and I would be able to thank her personally for creating a world that helped me escape my miserable life. I really wanted to meet her. She was my idol. I would be able to ask her if Sam could work at the Main House as well. I would tell her about his loyalty and commitment to Mindforder. I would do something, anything, because I couldn't bear the thought of never seeing him again.

I walked home wondering how Beatrix and Tom were feeling about being separated. They had been together since arriving on the Island.

I got indoors and finally kicked my hard shoes off as Sam went straight into the kitchen.

I stood still for a while and watched him standing at the fridge drinking a glass of water, and it suddenly hit me. I would choose him over the Main House.

I walked over to him and reached out my hand to touch his drinking arm.

He stopped moving and glanced at my hand, then back at his glass.

'Sam,' I said softly.

'Hmm,' was his reply.

I didn't really have anything else to say. My feelings for him were taking over my thoughts. I had spent every day with him for four months, and each day had felt like a lifetime. I loved being around him, sleeping next to him, and having him as my husband. I just often wished I was in his arms.

His eyes rolled up to look into mine. We held the stare. It seemed like a long time. I hoped he could read me. Know what I wanted.

I leant forward and gently kissed his shoulder.

He didn't move.

I lifted my head and kissed his neck.

He didn't move.

My stomach was shaking inside. The vibration had reached the back of my throat. I was running on fear and excitement. I was like an addict, completely out of control of everything. My Angel status didn't stand a chance. No part of me stood a chance. I no longer cared about anything except him. I just wanted to feel every single part of him touching every single part of me. The consequences would have to wait.

The heat of my mouth so close to his neck was pushing back into my face. I moved closer to his cheek and placed my lips there. It was my last shaky attempt to make him move. He had to move. He had to do something. Say something, at least. I needed to know if he wanted me.

'Maggie,' he whispered. 'We can't. It's forbidden.'

'I can't control it,' I whispered back, my lips refusing to leave his cheek.

'Yes, you can.' His voice was breathy and low.

'I don't want to,' I admitted, my tone matching his.

There was a moment of silence. Neither of us moved an inch.

I felt a tear escape my eye and roll down my cheek.

Sam's face slowly moved until his mouth met my lips.

It was our second kiss, but this time it felt different. Our connection felt exciting, dangerous, and I was completely lost in him at once.

Sam moved his arm so that he could place the glass down on the kitchen side. He then placed both his hands on my face and held me close to him. His thumb gently swiped my falling tear away. His lips were filled with passion as he kissed my mouth, my face, and my neck. Right there in that moment, submissive Sam was gone. He took control of the situation.

There was no turning back. Not for either of us. We had crossed the line, and we had no excuses we could use to mask that fact.

He picked me up, and my legs willingly wrapped around his waist. He carried me into the bedroom, all the while kissing me, never leaving my mouth.

I was carefully placed on the mattress. He pulled his top off over his head, and I quickly leant up onto my elbows.

'Help me with my dress.'

He leaned over me and unbuttoned the back and helped me to pull it off. It got a bit stuck around my head. I came out of my dress with static hair, a flushed face, and a grin.

Sam was smiling back at me. He breathed out a laugh. 'Are you okay, Maggie?'

'I'm fine,' I said softly.

He stood up straight and pulled off his bottoms. He watched me remove my underwear.

We were ready for bed, but not in our usual way.

He placed his body over mine, and I held on to his arms.

'Are you sure about this, Maggie?'

I nodded.

His eyes smiled down at me. 'You stop me if it doesn't feel right.'

'It feels right, Sam.'

* * *

I woke up and just for a few seconds everything was normal, but then I remembered what I did with Sam during the night.

I turned my head to look over at him. He was still asleep. I felt the corners of my mouth curl up.

I pulled the covers off me and sat up with my legs hanging out of the bed. I looked down at my bare skin. I closed my eyes for a moment and revisited all of the parts Sam had touched. I opened my eyes and realised that there wasn't one part of me that he hadn't touched.

I stood up and went into the bathroom. After I had used the toilet, I stepped into the shower and switched it on. I waited at the back, with my arm stretched out, until I felt the water turn lukewarm on my hand, then I stepped forward and stood beneath the spray. I opened my mouth and allowed the liquid to pour inside as I tilted my head upwards. The water drained away from my lips and my eyes. I lowered my head and rested my arms on the wall in front of me. I thought about my night with Sam.

I didn't know how he would feel. I was pretty sure he wouldn't report me, but would he still want me? Was it a one off? Would he wake filled with regret?

I had no regrets. None.

I smiled, as I could still feel him. The water was washing away his scent but not my memory.

I crossed my arms and placed my hands around the back of my shoulder blades and closed my eyes. I was standing there, hugging myself, pretending that he was holding me.

I didn't have to pretend for long.

Sam stepped into the shower behind me and placed his hands on my hips and his mouth on top of my shoulder.

I felt relief fill every fibre of my being. I lowered my arms, opened my eyes, lifted my head, and leant it back into him. His lips kissed my neck, then moved over to my cheek.

The water was spraying over my body and hitting him in the face, but he didn't seem to care.

I moved sideways and placed my hands on the side wall. His body followed mine.

Sam was leaning over my arched back, kissing along my shoulder. I lifted my arm up and backwards to touch his head. I tightened my fingers on his hair and pushed myself back into him.

'You want to do it like this, Maggie?' he asked gently, in between kisses.

'Yes.'

I watched his hands move along my arms. His fingers gripped mine on the wall. His mouth was on my back. I kissed his hand and, before either of us had started, I knew that we were dishonouring Mindforder. Ignoring everything that Buddy had said. Going against all that we were supposed to be. Neither of us stood a chance of being honoured. I was pretty sure of that, but it wasn't until the day that Sam was punished that I was completely sure.

14

Mackenzie

I had been working at Moreton Hall for nine weeks, not that I was counting. Adam was. He reminded me daily of my time there by putting up some sort of countdown calendar in his window each morning. I think it was his way of celebrating my work journey. Sam was the only guest we had, and he wasn't exactly a joy to be around. I had more fun when George was there, when he wasn't being all grown up and serious, that is.

It was the start of winter, and the old house was doing well to keep out the draughts. I spent a lot of time indoors, mostly in the kitchen or office, but every so often I'd go for a walk around the grounds or sit by the lake. Sam would as well, but I made sure I didn't let that stop me. He didn't own the place, probably could afford to. I tried to keep my distance from him, mostly, only because he was moody. He didn't speak much to me anyway. He mainly just stared at me. I was never quite sure what he was thinking when he went into stare mode. We did some small talk. Well, I did, but it never went down well. Sam definitely wasn't the small talk type, and I wasn't a fan either.

George constantly reminded me that we had to have patience with our guests. They had been through a lot, and we were there to help them.

I was there to pour the tea and serve the food. Sometimes, it seemed that George forgot that.

Victoria never forgot that. I always knew my place around her. Everyone did. She ran a tight ship.

I'd often left a cup of tea on top of the oak chest of drawers in Sam's room while he was in the shower. He seemed to like taking showers around 11 a.m.

I placed the white mug down on his chest of drawers and wondered where he was. I couldn't hear the shower coming from his en suite.

He never used to have a side bathroom, but once he was no longer classed as a red alert, he got upgraded. That was before I had arrived.

George had taught me about the traffic light system they had in place. Sam was somewhere between yellow and green.

I went over to the window to look out at the windy day. I always liked the wind. I found it refreshing. I watched the tips of the trees swaying, and then I jumped as Sam's bathroom door opened and he walked into the bedroom.

Sam froze. He glanced at me, then at the cup of tea on the side, and then back at me.

I was trying to avoid the fact that his chest was bare and his bottom half was wrapped in a white towel.

I thought it best to say something. 'I'm sorry. I thought you were somewhere else.'

He glanced back at the bathroom. 'I was.'

'I didn't know you were in there.' I had to clarify.

'Thanks for the tea,' he said politely, then took a sip.

He had a strange way of making me feel both comfortable and uncomfortable at the same time.

He walked towards me, then stopped suddenly and sat down on the end of his bed, facing me.

I shifted my feet a bit and rubbed my thumb. 'I'll leave you to it.'

'Sit down,' he said casually. 'Stay for a while.'

I don't know why, but I did. I sat up the top end of his bed, pulled his pillow up, and rested my back on it.

He raised his eyebrows and corners of his mouth. 'Make yourself comfortable there, Mackenzie.'

I watched him gulp down some tea, then place the cup on the floor by his feet.

George had told me to just let Sam speak anytime he wanted to, because he didn't speak that often. I tried to stay silent, but that wasn't in my nature. I had to speak.

'What are you up to today?'

He breathed out a slight laugh. 'Ah, you know, thinking of going skiing.'

'It's not a stupid question. You still do stuff here.'

He shrugged. 'Watch a film, maybe.'

'Which types do you like watching?'

'Romance.'

I laughed. 'You're a man.'

He looked directly at me. 'Are you being sexist, Mackenzie?'

God, he was right. I sounded that way. 'Sorry.'

'What type of film do you like?'

'Action,' I said happily. 'I'm not into romance or anything mushy that makes me cry.'

He raised his eyebrows as he looked down at his feet. 'Love makes you cry?'

Oh God, what was I starting to sound like. 'No. I just prefer to feel uplifted rather than feel sad and walk around all day projecting my glumness like some sort of Debbie downer.'

His head shot up from the floor. The softness in his face had gone. 'Don't say that. Don't attach a woman's name to a negative term.'

'I didn't mean it like that. It's just what people say.'

'They shouldn't say it. It's not right. Women's names should not be used as labels for things that are negative, and anyway, it's okay to feel sad, Mackenzie. There's nothing wrong with showing emotion. If you feel down, you feel down. It shouldn't be silenced by a label. Don't let anyone put you in a box like that.'

'Wow, you lot from Mindforder really are feminists,' I blurted out.

'You lot,' he huffed out. He shook his head slightly and brushed his hands on the towel covering his legs. 'We didn't use the word feminist. Besides, noticing that women's names are often attached to negativity does not make you a feminist. It makes you awake.'

'I've never noticed.'

He nodded. 'Clearly.'

'It's not that much of a big deal. It's just a small thing in the grand scheme of things.'

His head shook slightly. He looked over at me. 'You have to watch the small stuff, Mackenzie. It's designed to be sly, sneaky, to slip under the radar so that it's almost invisible, but it does a lot of damage. Have you never noticed that when it's something positive, nine times out of ten, a man's name is attached to it, and when it's negative, a woman's name is attached. There's a reason for that.'

'There is?'

He nodded. He sat up straight. His eyes were sharp, alert. He still had the gentleness about his face, but it was also filled with seriousness. His hands were shaking slightly, as though he were running on adrenalin.

'Yes,' he told me. 'Labels are created to shut women down. Shut down their emotions, shut down their strengths, and most definitely shut up their mouths. You have to be careful. Labels are stamped on women to ridicule them into silence. To put them back inside their box. Women have been fighting for way too long to be heard, to be seen, to be respected. You can't let them shut you down now. Look out for all the sugar-coated shite out there, Mackenzie.'

'Did they teach you that in Mindforder?'

'Yes, but that's neither here nor there. This isn't about Mindforder. It's about all the sneaky ways out there designed to stop women from becoming equal. You shouldn't have to join Mindforder to know what's happening. We should all know. We should all help to fight this. Women shouldn't be second-class citizens.'

'Nobody should.'

He seemed to settle a bit. His hands had stopped shaking.

'Your fight isn't over, Mackenzie,' he said softly. 'There are countries where women aren't even treated like humans. They are controlled and beaten. Some don't even own their own name. That's another good reason why people in our country shouldn't use women's names as derogatory terms. We're one of the front runners. Those countries behind us can see how far we have come in our fight, and that can help to inspire them to keep moving forward. Women should inspire other women, not help to put them down. If you all came together, you would be such a force. How will women ever be equal if they don't stand together?'

'You're very passionate about equality.'

He nodded. 'There are too many people fighting for equality, Mackenzie. It's not right. Everyone should be treated the same, and no one should have to fight for that.'

I had a sudden thought. 'I've never actually done anything to help the fight for women's equality.'

'Well, you can start by never attaching a woman's name to something negative again. And don't ever allow anybody to ridicule you into silence or make you feel bad about expressing any kind of emotion. You're not a Stepford Wife, you're a human being.'

I nodded my agreement, even though I didn't know what a Stepford Wife was. I made a mental note to find out later on and to also talk to Adam's mum about equality.

I knew Malorie used to go on marches. Perhaps I could be part of a demonstration. I felt inspired. Malorie would know loads more about unfairness than Sam. She had spoken to me about her life.

'I'm a black woman who was raised in care homes in one of the poorest communities in London. I have had to fight all my life, and there isn't a person in this world that will ever hold me back,' she told me.

She went on to tell me that she was also a single parent of an adopted white child, who became disabled and suffered with depression for a year, and that she had faced more stigmas in her life than she'd had hot dinners.

I always had a great admiration for Malorie. She worked as a CEO for some tech company in London that had started off small and had then hit the big time, which had something to do with apps. The man who started the business made all of his ten staff members just as rich as him, and they were all given senior roles. It was the one place in the world where she had found her equality. Everyone was treated fairly there. She offered me a job at her company once. Adam said I should try it out, but I couldn't see myself sitting in an office all day. I didn't ever see myself serving tea all day either, but here I was.

I snuggled back into Sam's pillow, getting comfortable. 'Can I ask you something?'

Sam smiled to himself. 'You don't normally ask.'

He had a point.

'What do you want to ask me, Mackenzie?'

‘If you’re so big on equality, why were you happy to stay in Mindforder? They don’t treat everyone the same. They completely flipped the equality between men and women. They make men the second-class citizens.’

He took a deep breath before he spoke. ‘They do that for a reason. It’s to help raise women’s self-worth.’

I scoffed. ‘And the only way they think they can do that is by belittling men?’

‘I wasn’t belittled.’

I nodded. ‘I read some stuff on Mindforder. You were.’

‘It’s not what you think, Mackenzie.’ He gazed over at the window. ‘Men have entitlement drip fed into them from birth. Society is so used to it, we don’t even know we’re doing it. We raise our boys to be protectors, to be the stronger sex. We’re programmed from childhood in different ways to girls. All that pink and blue crap. Some of that data makes us subconsciously feel more powerful than women.’

I nodded.

Sam started to play with his fingers. ‘Mindforder decided that the way forward for women was to lower the entitlement in men. They do that by having them live like someone without any rights, but we did have rights, you see. We had the right to choose that life to help women.’

‘And what’s with all the babies being born there?’

‘We figured we’d raise the children with equality and positivity. We’d show the world how it’s done. Did you know that growing inside a womb in a negative environment can impact your mental state of mind before you even enter the world?’

I shook my head. ‘You think an unborn baby can pick up on that?’

‘It’s true.’

He looked quite adamant. I didn't want to push the subject. Sam was no longer a member of Mindforder, but that had not stopped a lot of their beliefs staying with him.

I got up from the bed. I had work to do. I liked deep conversations, but I wasn't used to having them with many people. Whenever George wasn't at work, he liked to talk about sport or music. My relationship with Adam was pretty light too. We giggled a lot and watched movies on our laptops together on our windowsills.

Sam was a whole new character in my life. Even when his eyes were in serious mode, I could see how lost he was. There was something about him that was endearing. I found myself enjoying his company, but now I needed a break.

I leaned down at his feet and picked up the cup. His hand reached out and tucked a hair behind my ear that had become loose from my ponytail. I gazed up at him.

His eyes smiled softly at me. He pointed towards my ear. 'Sorry,' he mumbled.

I stood up and tried not to smile. I headed for the door, where my tea trolley was. I turned to say something, but I stopped when I saw the scars running across his bare back. I froze.

Sam shuffled on the bed and looked over his shoulder at me. I think he knew I was just standing there staring at him.

'Are you looking at my scars, Mackenzie?' His voice was soft and low, almost broken but unashamed.

'Oh God, Sam.' I felt tears appear in my eyes. 'I'm so sorry.'

He gave me a slight smile. 'It's okay.'

I shook my head. 'No, it's far from okay. Did they do that to you?' I was still staring at the long slash lines going in different directions across his back.

He waved me over towards him.

I slowly approached the other side of the bed. He reached out his hand and took mine, pulling me across the mattress, closer to him.

I knelt on the bed and flung my arms around his neck and hugged him.

'It's okay, Mackenzie,' he said softly. 'Thought you might have read about it in my file.'

'I haven't got that far yet,' I admitted.

I wasn't much of a reader, and when I had reached a part where it was all psychobabble, I had drifted away.

We moved apart and looked at each other. He reached out his hand and wiped away a falling tear from my cheek.

'Do you want me to tell you about it?' he asked.

'Do you want to relive that?'

He shrugged. 'It is what it is.'

I placed one hand on his back and gently stroked his scars. I watched him close his eyes and take a deep breath.

'Why would they do this to you?' I almost cried again. I could feel his past pain, his present pain, and I didn't like what I was feeling. What had this man been through? I knew that I needed to finish reading his file, but now I didn't want to.

He opened his eyes and turned his face towards mine. 'There was this man called Ross.'

15

Maggie

I wasn't having the best day. I stared glumly at the worksheets in front of me. They were sprawled out on the, already untidy, desk.

Jenny wasn't the neat type. Her office was a mess, which was why I refused, to myself, to call it my office.

I couldn't get the argument I had in the morning with Sam out of my head. It carried on from the night before. It wasn't much of a row because he knew he wasn't allowed to argue with me, plus, he kept his voice calm and avoided eye contact a lot, but he had stuff he wanted to say, so he said it.

He had told me that we had to stop touching each other. That it had gone too far. That we were breaking the rules, and that we should care about that fact.

He refused to touch me from that moment onwards. He told me that if I couldn't be strong, then he would be strong for the both of us.

His face was so determined. Mine just looked how I felt, deflated.

I missed his touch already, but I understood where he was coming from. He was right. What we had been doing was wrong, and we had to stop.

I wanted to be annoyed with him for rejecting me, but I was too busy being annoyed at myself for falling out of line, and falling in love.

I was pretty sure I did love him. I was also pretty sure I had shown my Angel status no respect.

I felt torn. I got on so well with Sam. We just connected and hardly ever disagreed. He made me feel safe and warm and needed. Even during our dispute, he looked even more submissive than usual, and I was sure he did that on purpose so that I didn't feel threatened at all.

Annie rushed into the Larder, jolting me out of my daydream. 'Maggie, you need to come.'

I looked up from my desk to see that her face was drawn, and her expression fearful. Her voice was shaky, as were her hands.

'What's wrong, Annie?'

She waved me towards the door. 'Quickly. He's about to be punished.'

I jumped out of my chair to approach her. 'Who is?'

'Sam.'

I felt the blood drain from my face. 'Sam? What for?' I managed to ask.

'Defiance.'

* * *

By the time I had reached the field, Sam had already been tied to a post. He was on his knees with his arms wrapped around the wooden stake in the ground. His head was twisted sideways, resting against the wood. His back was bare. The full force of the strong sunlight glared down upon his unprotected skin.

I had seen that post before, but I never thought much about its purpose. It was just a wooden pole in the ground over towards the trees. It had a short post, not as wide, resting horizontally across it about a quarter of the way down from the top. The whole post was only about four foot high.

Sam's hands were resting on top of the smaller post, tied by rope. I saw the large knot as soon as I ran over to him.

Everyone was standing around in the near distance over by the hut, watching silently. Mary-Lynn was up front, the closest to Sam. It took me a few seconds to process the fact that she was holding a whip in her hands.

Annie went over to stand with her husband as soon as we had arrived.

I was alone with Sam. He had his back to the onlookers. I was staring straight at them.

'What are you doing?' I cried out to Mary-Lynn.

Sam looked up at me as I dropped to my knees in front of him. I grabbed the rope.

Mary-Lynn called out to me, 'Maggie. Step away.'

Sam whispered to me, 'Get back, Maggie.'

I was still holding the rope. 'What is this?' I asked Mary-Lynn. 'What's happening here?'

From out of the shadow of the hut stepped a woman. It took me a moment to see it was Rochelle. Some people parted to let her through. She stood by Mary-Lynn's side, then turned so that everyone could see her.

'Sam is to be punished for his crime,' she told her audience.

I felt Sam's fingertips touch mine. 'Maggie, go now,' he whispered through gritted teeth.

I glanced at him. His eyes were stern, unrecognisable to me. I looked back over at Mary-Lynn. She had a slight twisted grin. I turned my attention to Rochelle.

'What crime?' I demanded. Did they know about us?

'He disobeyed a wife,' said Rochelle loudly.

A few gasps wafted through the small gathering.

I stood up. 'Who?'

Joanne stepped forward. 'Me,' she announced coldly.

I already knew what Sam had done. It was obvious, but I asked anyway. 'How?'

'He watered my husband,' she replied.

I felt Sam's fingers tug at mine. I glanced down at him. I could tell he was warning me.

I could feel my stomach churning. I practically screamed at Rochelle, 'She's abusing her husband.'

The crowd gasped again. Some whispers passed between them before they fell silent to find out what would be said next.

Annie gave me a look that was trying to silence me. I ignored her.

Rochelle turned to face Joanne. 'Abusing?'

'I've seen her,' I said. 'She tips his water away.'

Sam's fingers tightened on mine. 'No, Maggie,' he said softly.

I spoke to the crowd. 'Isn't that a crime?'

Nobody moved.

Rochelle waited for Joanne to speak.

Joanne shuffled slightly. Her face was filled with authority, but I could sense her fear.

Rochelle questioned her, 'Why?'

'Because he needs it,' Joanne replied. 'He is weak. He is failing the Island. Failing our family.'

Rochelle turned back to me. 'I know you haven't been here as long as the rest of us, Maggie, but you should know by now that sometimes we all need some help with our discipline.' She turned to the crowd for confirmation.

They obediently nodded her way.

I was shocked at the way everyone was reacting. 'Have you seen Ross?' I asked. 'He looks like he's about to die. How is that helping any of us?'

'Ross is in the Ward being taken care of,' said Mary-Lynn.

'He collapsed,' whispered Sam.

I yelled out, 'Only because he is now so ill, thanks to her.' I pointed at Joanne, and I didn't care how defiant I was acting.

I wasn't the confrontational type. I had always been the quiet one. The one who took the crap and never answered back. My outburst was against the person I was, but Sam was on his knees before me, tied to a post, and Mary-Lynn was holding a whip, and I knew exactly what was coming next. I just didn't know what I could say or do to save my husband from a beating.

'It's none of your business what a wife does with her husband,' said Mary-Lynn.

'It's all of our business,' I told her. 'We're a family,' I told them all. 'We're supposed to support each other. This whole place is about a high level of positivity. How is killing Ross and beating Sam going to help with that?'

I thought I gave a good argument, but I wasn't used to defending myself, except for raising my arms to protect my head from a punch.

Rochelle appeared calm. 'Maggie, this is how we keep the level of discipline so high here. We have no choice. Sometimes people have to be reminded of their duty.'

'Can't we just deport the ones not doing a good job?' I asked. I thought it was a reasonable thing to do. 'There are loads of people in the villages who would give anything to come here and spread positivity. Swap them. It would be more productive than this.'

Mary-Lynn lowered her head and laughed to herself.

Rochelle ignored her and continued to speak to me, and her audience. 'That's not how things work here, Maggie. We have our own rules, and they have been working fine for many years. Now, step away from your husband.'

She watched me hesitate. They all did.

‘It’s for his own good,’ she added. ‘He will thank us.’

I was pretty sure he wouldn’t.

‘Go, Maggie,’ Sam whispered.

‘Maggie, you are being defiant,’ said Rochelle. She sounded cold. Her patience had disappeared. She had explained the situation to me. She was making it quite clear that she was done talking.

Annie waved me towards her, but nobody but me noticed her slight action.

Mary-Lynn tapped the whip on her hand. ‘You can be punished with him, if you like,’ she told me.

Rochelle remained silent.

It was then that I knew I could be tied to a post at any minute. Sam’s fingers got my attention. He glared at me. He had so much anger in his eyes. I had never seen him look that way before.

‘Go away,’ he told me. ‘Now.’

I didn’t know what to do. I couldn’t just stand there and watch him get flogged. I couldn’t move. My body felt frozen. My legs had turned to jelly, and my voice had disappeared.

Annie approached Rochelle. ‘May I have your permission to fetch Maggie? She can stand with me. She just needs some guidance. I can help her with that.’

Rochelle thought for a second, then gave her a slight nod.

I watched Annie approach. She stopped in front of me. She had her back to the crowd. She offered her hand. ‘Come with me, Maggie,’ she said softly. Her voice was warm and caring.

‘I can’t move,’ I whispered.

She touched my hand. The touch forced my body to wake.

‘Just walk away with me,’ she said gently. ‘Just keep looking at me, Maggie.’

I had reached Annie's husband at the same time the first crack of the whip hit Sam's back.

I froze as Sam's yell filled the area.

Annie lifted my chin. 'You watch, Maggie. Turn and watch. It will be much worse for you both if you don't,' she whispered.

I felt her turn my body around to the direction that everyone was facing. I looked just in time to see the second strike. It ripped through me.

Annie held me tightly. She could, no one was watching us. All eyes were on Sam's open wounds.

He stopped making a sound after the fifth cut. He was slumped there lifelessly. A part of me wondered if he had died.

'He'll survive,' whispered Annie. 'He'll be stronger after.'

Sam was whipped by Mary-Lynn a total of ten times, not that I was counting. She even stopped at one point to have a drop of water and wipe her brow. She told the crowd that she found no joy in this part of her work, but the Island needed her to be strong.

She looked like she was enjoying her job to me.

When it was over, Rochelle told everyone to go home, and then she swiftly left the scene. I had no idea what was to happen next. Nobody even looked my way. They all quietly departed. Going home for their dinner, no doubt. Even Mary-Lynn had nothing to say before she walked away.

Annie was the last to leave. She gave me my instructions.

'You can untie him now, Maggie. You have to take him to the Ward to be treated. No one is allowed to help you. If you can't carry him there, he will have to stay here until he can move himself. It's not advisable. He will get an infection. Find a way to move him. Use a cart if you can't hold him up. Just move him. Get him there. Do not ask anyone for help. If anyone helps you move your husband, they will be punished. Do you understand?'

I understood perfectly. I nodded.

She kissed me on the cheek and hurried away.

I turned to face Sam's bleeding back. I told myself to wake up. Get a grip. Move. Do something. Anything.

I quickly ran to the tap to fill my cup with water, and then I made my way over to Sam.

I knelt before him.

'Sam,' I said softly. 'Sam, can you move?' I didn't want to ask him if he was all right because it was obvious that he wasn't.

Sam groaned.

I tried to lift his head and water his mouth.

He took a sip.

'Take some more,' I told him.

He tried, but couldn't.

I tipped some water into my hand and gently splashed his cheeks. I threw the rest away and began to untie his hands. It wasn't easy. The rope was tight, and it left my fingers red and sore.

Sam flopped down even further once his hands were released. I tried to lift him, but he was heavy. I was scared to touch his back. I didn't know how to carry him. I looked around for a cart. There was one near the hut.

'I'll be right back,' I told him.

I ran for the cart and grabbed its wooden handles. I could feel the splintered wood pressing into my skin. The four wheels were old and rusty, making the cart hard to move. The whole thing had seen better days, but was obviously still useful for local jobs. I had no idea how I was going to manoeuvre it all the way to the Ward with Sam on top of its old, dirt-ingrained wood. I just knew I had no choice. It took me a while to push it over to Sam's lifeless body.

'Sam, get up.' I sounded forceful, but I knew I had to be. He had to move. He had to help me move him.

I tugged at his arm. I threw it around my neck and placed my body beneath the side of his chest.

He was groaning.

'Come on, Sam,' I urged.

I could feel him trying. He was trying to stand, but his legs were weak.

'You need to get on the cart.'

I walked forward a step. It was so hard. I was carrying a dead weight, and my knees were giving way. I fell to them, and then I struggled to lift myself with Sam.

'Sam, please, help me.'

I could feel the tears sitting in my eyes, but I refused to let them fall. Now was not the time. Sam needed medical help, and I couldn't call for an ambulance. No one was coming to help him. I was the only one who could help him. I had to be strong. I had to find more body strength. I had to keep my mind from having a meltdown.

'Come on, Sam. We need to get to the Ward. No one's allowed to help us. You have to move.'

Sam's weight lightened a touch. He was doing it. He was mustering all of his strength to move himself onto the cart.

My head fell down with his body as he collapsed close to the front wheel. I adjusted my position and shoved him sideways. He flopped over onto the cart. I lifted and curled his legs. One was hanging off the end, but I knew it wouldn't be in my way. I leant on the side of the cart to support myself as I caught my breath. I could see the blood dripping into the cracks in the wood.

I glanced down at the blood on my hands. It blended in with the rope sores on my fingers, and the splinters in my palms. I wiped them down my dress and immediately felt the sting of the splinters rub against the material. I gritted my teeth, then looked down at Sam's shredded back. I knew not to complain about how I felt.

'Okay, Sam. Let's do this.'

I moved around to the worn handles and lifted the cart. I pushed it forward, but it didn't budge. The wheels were on the grass. It wasn't helping. I knew I couldn't turn the cart, so I pressed my heels down and pulled instead. It moved an inch. I tugged again. Another inch. I was already sweating.

The sun was starting to set over the field, but the heat was still strong. The air smelled musty and felt humid. I could feel my lungs fighting to breathe.

Sam was still. I was worried about shock. I didn't know whether or not to cover him with something. I didn't want anything sticking to his open wounds. I left him bare.

I took a couple of slow and steady breaths, and then I pulled the cart again. Inch by inch, I made it over towards the hut and onto the pathway.

The cart moved slightly easier once on the flatter surface, but the pathways were made of fine gravel embedded in concrete paving, so it wasn't a smooth journey.

My stomach was tight. I felt sick. My head was hot. I felt dizzy. My legs had a life of their own. They were moving. Just moving. My arms ached, and my shoulders were in so much pain. They were burning on the inside.

I stopped a few times. Caught my breath. Checked on Sam. Channelled my energy. Prayed. I prayed that my body wouldn't fail Sam. I prayed for the strength I needed to stop me from fainting. I prayed for help.

There was hardly any sun left in the sky by the time I had reached the Ward. I dropped the handles of the cart and ran inside to fetch the doctor.

The air conditioning hit me, making my head swirl. I could feel my skin start to burn. I looked straight down the hut. The doctor wasn't there, but the nurse was.

He took one look at me, and I saw the concern flash in his eyes. It stayed there for less than a second.

'Where is he?' he asked.

I pointed towards the doorway.

He ran outside and I followed closely.

It was apparent that the nurse was allowed at this point to help me carry Sam inside. We each had one of his arms draped over us. We practically dragged him over to a nearby bed. His feet were scraping along the floor.

'On his front,' the nurse told me.

We placed Sam down, not very gently, onto the mattress. I lifted his legs and tried to make sure he was in a comfortable position.

The nurse turned to me as I almost collapsed onto the floor at the foot of the bed.

'There's water by the door. Get some.'

Doubled over, I made my way towards the water cooler and grabbed my cup and filled it up under the tap. I drank it all in one go, then refilled my cup. I slid down to the floor. My legs had died. I poured the water over my head.

The nurse approached me. 'You have to go home now.'

I glanced up at him. He was slightly older than me. He had dark hair and dark eyes. He had a warm face, but it had been trained to look cold and uncaring. Every so often, a glimpse of his true personality shone through, but it lasted seconds. He knew his place, and he knew mine.

‘You are to return in three days to collect your husband. I’ll give you full instructions on how to continue his care when you come back. You are not permitted to visit him, so do not try.’

I had no words.

‘Have another cup of water before you leave,’ he said softly.

My eyes rolled over my shoulder towards the tap. I managed to turn slightly so that I could fill my cup without too much movement.

The nurse watched me sip the water.

He nodded down at me. ‘Take it with you.’

It was time to go. He was being polite about that fact.

I rolled onto my knees and used the water cooler to help me stand. It wobbled, so I let go. I looked the nurse straight in the eyes.

‘He will be okay,’ he told me quietly.

I glanced down the Ward and saw Ross curled up in a bed in the far corner. I then glanced over at Sam. He wasn’t moving or groaning, just bleeding. I looked down at my hands.

The nurse looked at them too. ‘Go home. Wash up. Come back in three days.’

I turned slowly. My body just about allowed me to move. I made my way back outside into the warm night. I stood on the pathway out front for a moment. I felt numb and completely alone.

16

Mackenzie

I reached Adam's front door. It was late. I was tired, worn through, in fact. Sam's backstory had drained me, and I needed to talk to someone. I knew I wasn't allowed to talk about him. I just wanted to talk to someone about anything that wasn't heavy or deep.

I looked at the intercom beside the dark-brown wooden door. Malorie had it installed along with many other gadgets that helped make Adam's life easier after his accident.

All the years I'd know him, and yet, I had never been inside his home. Why I was standing on his doorstep was beyond me. My feet just walked that way.

I pressed the brushed-chrome button on the white plate built into the brickwork.

It was silent, so I wasn't sure if it was working. I gazed into the tiny camera inside the contraption and jumped back when Adam's voice came through the speaker.

'Mac,' he questioned. 'You okay?'

'Hi, Adds. I just wanted to talk.'

I knew straight away I sounded weird. Normally, I would toss some grit at his window, and we would talk that way. Why wasn't I doing that now?

I felt my heart jolt slightly as the door suddenly clicked open. I paused for a second before reaching out my hand to push the door fully open.

I stepped inside the hallway and gently closed the door behind me. I heard it lock.

Adam's hallway looked bigger than mine. Definitely a lot less cluttered, and it seemed to be missing a wall. Our houses looked the same from the outside, but after Malorie's home improvements, their home wasn't anything like anyone's on the street.

I glanced at the stairs and wondered if that had been widened as well. It looked wider than ours. Maybe because it had polished wooden steps with a cream carpet down the middle. It looked lovely.

My eyes wandered over to the glass lift at the back of the hallway. It was wide enough for Adam's wheelchair and at least two people standing. It looked quite posh for a lift, with its chrome bars and white floor. I did spend a moment debating whether or not to use it.

I walked over to the bottom of the stairs and flipped off my shoes. Malorie's eyes caught my attention as they stared down at me from a framed enlarged photograph of her and Adam.

I smiled at the picture. Adam was only about six when it was taken. He looked so cute.

I checked underneath both my feet before attempting the cream carpet on the stairs. I was worried about leaving any footprints. It looked brand new. I couldn't be the one who ruined it. I wondered if that was the reason why Malorie had hung her picture right there, so that anyone about to make the climb would feel her glare boring into their soul. I could hear her voice inside my head, scolding me for any marks left behind.

I daren't risk it. I made my way up the stairs like a starfish. That plush carpet wasn't going to blame me for any wear and tear.

Once I had reached the top, I looked back down to see if my feet had left behind any sweat marks on the wooden parts. It looked okay. I tried not to laugh as I thought about my dad jogging around Malorie's house. It was obvious she was house-proud. My dad's trainers would not get a welcome.

I turned my head left and right to get my bearings. Adam's house mirror-imaged mine, so his bedroom should be right over there.

I got to the door that I presumed was his and knocked quietly.

'Come in, Mac,' he called out.

I opened the door to find him sitting at the foot of his rather large bed. He was wearing dark-blue pyjama bottoms and no top. God, his top half looked fit. I averted my eyes.

'Is everything all right, Mac?' he asked.

I was still standing in his doorway, trying not to stare at his muscles.

'Hi, Adds,' I said simply.

He raised his eyebrows. 'Hello.'

I shifted forward a touch. 'So, this is what your room looks like.'

He followed me with his eyes as I walked over to his desk. It appeared he was just as much a neat freak as his mum. Everything was tidy, uncluttered, crisp, and clean. It was quite the contemporary room and very white. It really did need a splash of colour, in my opinion.

I glanced at a photograph sitting by his laptop. Malorie was sitting on a hospital bed next to Adam's birth mum, Natasha. Adam was a baby in Natasha's arms. She had a flowery pink scarf wrapped around her bald head. She had a sweet face and a big smile.

Natasha had been in the same care home as Malorie at one point. They became best friends. Declared themselves sisters. They were the only family each of them had, that was until Adam came along. He only got to spend two months with Natasha before she died, but Malorie made sure he grew up knowing everything about her.

I went over to the window. I wanted to see my own bedroom window from his point of view.

I knew inside was an array of colours, a lot of clutter, and, what I liked to call, organised chaos. I smiled at my room. There was no way Adam would be able to manoeuvre his wheelchair around my floor.

Adam stayed quiet as I secretly assessed his bedroom. It was bigger than mine. He had two rooms knocked into one. I thought I had better stop house surveying and say something. I went over to him and sat down at his side.

'Were you about to go to bed?' I asked softly.

He gave a slight nod. 'It's late.'

'Malorie not home?' I asked, knowing that she wasn't because her car wasn't in the drive.

'She's working in London. She's due back tomorrow.'

Now I was the one giving a slight nod.

'You had a bad day, Mac?'

I lowered my head. 'Yes.'

He put his arm around me, and I rested my head down on his shoulder. I felt his head touch mine.

'Do you want a cup of tea?' he asked.

'No. I'm fed up with tea.'

I felt him breathe out a short laugh, and then his head lifted from mine.

'I've got hot chocolate,' he said.

I sat up straight and looked at him.

He nodded over to the corner of his room next to the door. There was a L-shaped kitchen worktop, white, of course, and on it was a coffee machine, white, the type you put a pod into. Underneath was a small fridge and a cupboard.

‘Sure,’ I said. I stood up and went over to the machine. There was a wooden box next to it that had three rows of pods inside. One row was hot chocolate. I took one out and placed it into the machine. I turned to Adam.

He was using his upper-body strength to lift himself backwards so that he could rest his back against his headboard.

‘Do you want one?’

He shook his head. ‘Cups are in the cupboard.’

I bent over and took out a white coffee mug and placed it under the machine, then stared at it for a while, trying to figure out how to turn the contraption on.

‘Close the door while you’re up, Mac.’

I gave up on the drink, closed the bedroom door, and went over to sit by his side. I ended up sliding down upon a lovely soft pillow. I curled up on my side and pretty much snuggled myself under Adam’s arm. He smelled like he had not long showered.

‘Tired, Mac?’

‘Hmm.’

He adjusted his position so that he was lower down. He rested his head upon mine, and I placed one hand on his chest.

‘Have you had a good day, Adds?’ I yawned out.

‘I have,’ he replied, sounding more awake than me.

‘Tell me about it.’

I closed my eyes, heard the word *tour*, and then I drifted off to sleep.

* * *

I woke to find myself still hugging Adam’s chest. It was a first. A lot of firsts. First time in his house. First time in his room. First time in his bed. First time falling asleep in his arms. I felt quite relaxed, apart from the fact that I had fallen asleep in my clothes. My jeans weren't comfortable at all. I really needed a shower and change of clothes. It suddenly dawned on me that I had to go to work, and I had no idea what the time was. I leant up to look over at the digital clock on the bedside cabinet.

I had one hour to get ready and get to work. I wondered if George would be home. I'd get to work a lot quicker if he drove me. That would be plan A. Go home, get washed and changed, and then call George.

Adam's eyes opened. He stared up at me.

I was leaning over him. 'Morning.' I smiled, then slapped my hand over my mouth. 'Oh no, I have morning breath.'

He smiled back at me.

It took me a moment to realise I was staring at him. For some reason, my eyes refused to move away from his.

He looked away first. He turned his head to see the time. 'You got work today?'

I groaned out a yes and sat up. I looked down at my jeans. 'Sorry I fell asleep, Adds.'

His hand gently touched my back. Then, it nudged me. 'Get to work, Mac, before you're late.'

I laughed to myself as I got off the bed. I rubbed my eyes and turned to see him lifting himself to sit up.

'Do you want to share some dinner with me tonight?' I asked, not knowing why I said that. 'I probably won't get back till about seven, but the chippy will be open.'

He grinned. 'How about I make you dinner.'

'Will it involve chips?'

He shook his head. 'Probably not. Probably involve salad.'

I shrugged. 'Salad is fine.' It was much better with chips.

'See you later then,' he said, watching me open the door.

I attempted to flatten my hair as I said goodbye.

'You look great,' he shouted out.

I met the stairs.

Malorie was at the bottom, and not just her picture. I knew I would look stupid walking down the stairs trying not to touch the carpet, so I acted like a normal person and stepped onto the soft pile.

'Good morning, Mackenzie.'

I smiled at her. 'Morning, Malorie. I fell asleep. I didn't mean to. It just happened.' I was starting to sound like a rambling idiot, so I stopped talking.

She picked up my shoes and handed them to me. I took them and tried to balance myself while putting them on while standing.

'Can I come to a demonstration with you one day?' I blurted out, heading for the door.

Malorie frowned. 'Demonstration?'

'Women's rights,' I added. I slowly punched the air.

Malorie laughed to herself. 'If you want, but I don't tend to march much these days. There are plenty of other ways you can help with our movement.'

I nodded. 'Will you email me some information, please. I've been asleep for far too long, and not just in Adam's bed.' I laughed, then quickly added, 'We didn't do anything. We just slept.' I felt the need to clarify, then it hit me. 'Tour?'

'Tour?'

I looked over at the stairs. 'Tour,' I repeated.

Malorie frowned.

I kicked off my shoes and ran up the stairs before Malorie had a chance to say anything.

I burst into Adam's room and came to a sudden stop. He was sitting on the side of the bed with his legs hanging down. He had just removed his pyjama bottoms.

He was just as shocked as me. He gasped and quickly grabbed his scrunched-up bottoms to cover his modesty. 'Mac!'

I decided it was in both our best interests if I didn't say anything about what had just happened. I went straight over to him and sat down at his side.

'Before I fell asleep, you said something about a tour.'

His brow wrinkled as he raised his eyebrows.

'What tour?' I asked.

'You do realise I'm sitting here naked, right?'

I looked him in the eyes. 'You have your pyjamas on your lap.'

He went to say something but then stopped.

'Tour?' I reminded him.

'We'll talk about it tonight.'

'You can't do that to me, Adds. I'll be wondering all day. That's not healthy.'

'Not healthy?'

I shook my head. 'You know I don't have any patience.'

'You're going to be late for work.'

'Tell me quickly.'

'I'd rather not.'

'Is it a lot to say?'

He shrugged and took a deep, reluctant breath. 'I'm a member of the AOP.' He knew I had no idea what that was. 'Academy of Poetry.'

'Oh, I thought drawing pictures was your job.'

'I'm a digital artist, illustrator, song writer, and poet. Although, poetry is more my hobby. Anyway, every three years, they pick five poets to take on tour. This time, I got picked. We get to travel around Europe, displaying our work at exhibitions.'

'That's a thing?' I asked.

He tilted his head and nodded. 'Yes, Mac. That's a thing.'

I smiled at him. 'Hey, well done. You got picked.'

He beamed proudly. 'Yes, I did.'

'I'm not surprised. I love all your poems that you put in the window. You're very talented.'

He blushed. 'Thank you.'

I had a sudden thought. 'How long will you be travelling around Europe for?'

His shoulders drooped. 'Six months.'

My shoulders drooped. 'Six months! That's a long time.'

'We visit a lot of countries.'

'When do you leave?'

'April.'

We sat in silence for a while. I didn't know what to say. I felt happy for Adam but sad for myself. I missed him already, and he hadn't left yet.

'Now you know why I wanted more time to talk to you about this,' he said quietly.

I swallowed hard. I could feel tears building, and they weren't welcome. I rolled them back and looked down at my hands. I could see them clenched together. I loosened my grip on myself and took a slow and steady breath. I was not about to let my sorrow mess with Adam's joy.

Adam put his arm around me. 'I'll miss you too.'

I could feel the heartache ripping through me. First he was talking about moving, and now travelling. Either way, he was leaving me, and it hurt. I had to cheer up, for his sake.

I turned to look at him. Before I could speak, he gently placed his hand on my cheek to catch a falling tear I had missed.

‘Oh, Mac,’ he whispered.

‘I’m okay,’ I lied.

I was about to say something else when he leant over and kissed me on the mouth. I was surprised. I had no idea he was going to do that. I suddenly felt every part of me refusing to pull away. It felt so good. He felt so right. Morning breath had gone right out the window.

He slowly backed away and lowered his head. He looked as though he didn’t know what to say.

I didn’t know what to say. Come back, sprung to mind. Let’s get back in bed, was another thought. Please, never leave me, my heart said.

‘You’re going to be late,’ he mumbled.

I stood up and walked over to the door. I was worried he was now regretting the kiss. Friends shouldn’t kiss. Everyone knows that. It ruins the relationship. What if we were now ruined? What if he was no longer my friend? Could I be his friend and his girlfriend? I wanted to be. Right there and then, I knew I wanted to be.

‘Am I still invited for salad?’ I asked sheepishly.

He smiled at me. ‘You’re invited for everything.’

17

I entered Moreton Hall to see George decorating a Christmas tree in the hallway. Now I knew why he wasn't answering my calls.

'That looks lovely, George,' I said, taking off my coat and scarf.

Sam walked out of a side door, glared at the tree, and then walked into the dining room. 'You're late, Mackenzie,' his voice echoed back.

'I've had my breakfast,' said George. He waved over at the kitchen door. 'Hurry up, before Victoria comes out of her meeting.' He then nodded towards her office.

I went straight to the kitchen, slung my things down on the table, washed my hands, and got the milk out of the fridge.

Sam made me jump as he appeared in the doorway between the kitchen and dining room.

'Do you need any help?' he asked nicely.

'Oh, thank you, but I'm okay.'

'It's only my breakfast you have to worry about this morning,' he told me.

'Oh, okay.' I caught my breath and turned to him. 'What would you like?'

He came in and sat down at the table, opposite my coat, scarf, woolly hat, and beige handbag.

'I'll eat here, if that's all right?'

I shrugged. 'That's fine.' I put the milk down in front of him. 'Cereal?'

He shrugged. 'Not fussed.'

I grabbed the box of cornflakes, a bowl and a spoon, and placed them all before him.

His eyes rolled down into his empty bowl. I wasn't sure if he wasn't hungry or was waiting for me to fill it for him.

I gave his navy dressing gown the once over. 'Are you planning on getting dressed today?'

He reached out for the cornflakes. 'After my shower.'

Oh yes, his shower time. I had forgotten myself for a moment there. Then, I remembered him half naked, standing in front of me, looking gorgeous. I moved my things and sat down next to him.

'What shall we do today?' I asked.

He tipped some cereal into his bowl while raising his eyebrows at the question.

'Would you like to go into town?' I asked. 'I can speak to Victoria. See what she says.'

He looked over at me. 'Go into town?'

I shrugged. 'Why not?'

'I don't think I'm allowed to play out.'

I laughed. 'Won't know unless we ask.'

He poured the milk into the bowl. He stayed silent.

'Or are you a flight risk?' I asked.

He almost laughed. 'Where am I going to go?'

'You have to leave here one day. Why not start getting used to the outside again.'

'I like not being part of the world,' he said quietly.

'You are a part of this world, Sam, whether you like it or not.'

'Rather not be,' he mumbled.

'That's it. I'm taking you out, Samuel Whittington.' I headed for the door. 'Eat your breakfast and take a shower. I'll meet you in the hallway.'

He looked up at me and grinned. 'And where might you be taking me Mackenzie Watson?'

'Twenty minutes up the road, in the next town, model railway village.'

'Model railway village?'

'Everyone loves tiny trains, and there's one you can sit on that takes you for a ride around the attraction.'

'Not everyone loves tiny trains. Besides, it's winter. It'll be closed.'

I shook my head. 'It's not. It's open for Christmas, and I should know because my uncle drives the mini train. So, we'll even get a free ride, if you're good.'

He laughed. 'If I'm good?'

'You'll love it.'

* * *

I spent the next half hour with George in Victoria's office begging, explaining, and negotiating Sam's day release.

George was completely on my side. He thought it would do Sam the world of good to experience a day out with a couple of people around his own age.

Victoria had called Lennie, and we had to wait until they had discussed the proposal.

It took a while, and a lot of persuading, as it wasn't the usual protocol, but in the end, she agreed, mostly because George was going to be with us at all times. Plus, it was only up the road.

We had a curfew of seven o'clock, and she told George to take some money from the petty cash for food and admissions.

Sam was surprised when I rushed into his room to tell him of our day trip. He grabbed his coat, gloves, and scarf, and wrapped himself up ready for the fresh, cold air outside.

George supplied him with one of his many woolly hats, which were piled up in the cloakroom.

Sam's mother had brought him warm outer clothes for the garden, but he was never out there long enough to need a hat.

I laughed at the red bobbly hat slouched over his mop of hair. He looked like a model on the front cover of a ski magazine. He thought he just looked stupid, but he didn't say it within earshot of George, because George took great pride in picking hats.

We all snuggled nicely into George's bright red Mini Cooper, and off we went.

I asked if they wanted to sing Ten Green Bottles, but they both declined, so I sang it anyway.

* * *

Breanstone Model Railway Village was painted on the vintage sign at the entrance to the attraction. It was the only attraction that Breanstone had. The small neighbouring town was only slightly bigger than Oswell. It was a quaint Norfolk attraction that was quite popular with the tourists during the summer months and only graced by the presence of the locals during the festive season, mostly because it had a rather nice Santa's Grotto.

The model railway village was fully kitted out for Christmas. There were twinkling lights everywhere, and each model village had snow and Christmas trees. There was even a Polar Express train. Candyfloss machines, hotdogs, and hot chocolate urns sat in wooden Alpine huts that helped bring in the punters. The market side was designed to look every bit as magical as the North Pole itself.

Uncle Bert, who was my mum's eldest brother, dressed as an elf every year to drive the mini train around the outskirts of the place, and he loved every minute of it. If ever there was a season built for him, this was it. He had been the driver since he was nineteen. His wife, May, was one of the owners of the railway village. Her father had created the whole thing, mainly for himself at the time, but then people came to enjoy his enchanting hobby, and the rest, as they say, is history.

I happily linked arms with Sam and George as we entered. George had the biggest smile spread across his face, and Sam's body tightened as I flung my arm through his.

I took no notice of either of them. It was Christmas, we were on a day trip, it was mid-week, so not many families about, and I just loved the place.

'Come on,' I said cheerfully. 'Let's get some candyfloss.'

George stuffed the admissions tickets into his jacket pocket and almost skipped us over to a sweet hut.

'Three bags, please,' he told the elf-girl behind the wooden counter.

Sam twisted his head to look around. 'Are we actually in the North Pole?' He laughed to himself as George handed him a plastic bag filled with pink and blue candyfloss.

I released the lads to take my own bag of sugary air.

'Hey, George,' called out a man.

We all turned to see Valentine, a man we used to go to school with, who was named after the day he was born on.

Valentine was waving only at George. He hurried his stocky body towards us.

'George, long time no see.' He glanced sideways at me. 'Hello, Mac.' He looked at Sam.

'This is my cousin, Sam,' I said quickly.

Valentine shook his hand and went back to ignoring us. 'George, you have to come and say hello to Meghan. She's just over here.'

George glanced at me and Sam.

'Go on,' I encouraged. 'We'll be fine. I'm going to take Sam to see the mini villages.'

George looked at Sam.

Sam nodded. 'We'll be fine.'

'Okay, see you in a bit,' said George.

I nudged Sam's arm. 'You better not run away,' I teased. 'George will kill me.'

Sam laughed. 'Why would I run away when there's so much fun to be had here.'

I squinted my eyes at him and saw a flash of joy wash over his normally serious face. His cheeks were already flushed from the crisp afternoon air. I couldn't help but smile at him. He looked so different to the man he was at Moreton Hall. He fitted in perfectly with every other visitor around us, especially with George's woolly hat snuggled to his head.

We made our way over to the miniature trains running around model villages and stopped at the small country village one. It kind of looked like home.

'I always wanted to be able to shrink and live in one of these houses,' I said, giggling to myself.

'Is that a fact?'

I stuffed a large clump of candyfloss in my mouth. 'Wouldn't you like to do that?' I mumbled through my melting food.

'What was that?' He laughed into my face. 'Only a dentist understands that language, you know.'

I swallowed. 'Would you like to become teeny tiny?'

Sam pointed over at the model village as a small train chugged by in front of us. 'What, to live in there?'

I nodded. 'Or there are other settings over there.' I pointed sideways. 'Coastal, city, mountain side. Take your pick.'

Sam nodded towards a thatched cottage at the back of the village in front of us. It had pink walls and was sitting on its own in the middle of a field. 'I like that one.'

'It will be quiet living there.'

He smiled warmly at me. 'Quiet is good.'

'Don't you want a bit of life?'

He simply shook his head. 'No.'

I looked over at the cottage. 'It is lovely.'

'I reckon it's got an open fireplace inside with a real fire burning.'

I giggled. 'That'll burn Santa's bum. Speaking of which, do you want to go and see Santa?'

Sam laughed. 'I'm not sitting on his knee.'

'But he gives out free presents. Last year I got a small bag of marbles.'

'I could do with some marbles. I think I lost mine a long time ago.'

I smiled at him as he playfully nudged my arm.

The tiny steam engine passed us by again.

'If I were teeny tiny, I would drive that,' said Sam.

'Do you want to go for a ride on the mini train. You won't be able to leave until you've been on it. It's the law around here.'

'Oh, is that so?'

I smiled and joined in with the Jingle Bells song playing on the speaker above us.

Sam lowered his head and ate his candyfloss. I wasn't sure if he was embarrassed by my singing or just enjoying a moment by himself.

I led him through the model villages. We stopped at each one and chatted about which home would be the best one to live in if we could shrink ourselves.

He pointed out a big white house in one village and told me that it looked like his house in Ireland where he grew up.

'Will you ever go back there?' I asked.

He shrugged. 'Not sure.'

I pointed at the village. 'At least the villages can give you some home ideas.'

He nodded and smiled happily. I'd not seen him relax before. He was actually enjoying himself. I felt quite proud of myself. Victoria would be pleased.

Sam turned to me as a cold gentle breeze blew past us. He reached out and tucked away a strand of my hair. That was the second time he had come so close to touching my face. He adjusted my bright yellow woolly bobble hat so that my ears were covered, and he projected the warmth in his gentle eyes down into mine.

I smiled back at him, and, to my surprise, he started to sing along to the Santa Baby song playing around us.

We both laughed before he could finish the next line. He bent out his elbow and offered me his arm. I slipped mine through his, and we walked arm in arm over to Uncle Bert.

'Hello, darling. Thought you might be down the weekend,' he said merrily.

Everything Uncle Bert said came out merry. He seemed to be in a constant state of happiness. He always wore a smile and had no need for the red circles stamped on his cheeks because they were always flushed anyway. Still, he was playing his elf part, and rosy cheeks came with the package.

'I brought my friend, Sam. He could only come today, so here we are.'

Uncle Bert beamed a smile at Sam. 'Well, in that case, hop aboard, Sam. You can't leave here without this experience. It's the law.'

Sam breathed out a laugh. 'Oh, okay,' he said politely.

'Come on, Sam,' I said, tugging him. We walked along the red-and-black mini steam engine and climbed inside an empty open-topped carriage. It just about fitted us both in. Our knees collided, and Sam opened his legs so that mine could sit in between his. We were practically joined. I could feel the warmth of his body through his jeans pouring into my woolly tights. I felt instantly cosy.

Light snow started to fall. We both looked up, smiling and welcoming its appearance.

I watched the cold air escaping his mouth.

I stated the obvious. 'It's turning colder now.'

He leaned forward and placed his gloved hands on my cheeks to warm my face.

He was being so lovely.

The train jolted us as it started to move. Sam removed his hands and sat back to lean against the cold wood. Uncle Bert blew his whistle and both Sam and I laughed.

The ride only blew more cold air our way, but neither of us cared. We were too busy laughing, and I was also pointing out sights and taking some pictures with my phone. Sam even smiled in one. We waved to George as the train passed by the back of the Christmas market area.

George was drinking hot chocolate and chatting with his friends. He laughed when he saw us and waved back.

I took some pictures of him, then put my phone away in my bag.

Sam laughed. 'This is the best journey I've ever had.'

I smiled to myself at just how happy he was.

He waved me forward towards him as we passed by Santa's Grotto.

I leant forward to listen to what he had to say.

He tugged my coat so that I was closer to him, and then he hugged me.

His warm body was wrapped around mine, cradling me in his arms. I felt safe and warm and happy to be there. I was no longer in Breanstone, on Uncle Bert's mini train, I was just there, in Sam's strong hold. I wrapped my arms around him.

'Thank you, Mackenzie,' he whispered.

I closed my eyes for a moment.

Sam gently pulled away and sat back to glance out at the view again.

I had no words. I was somewhere far away, still wrapped in his warmth.

* * *

We got back to Moreton Hall at exactly seven o'clock, as instructed. Victoria was waiting for us in the hallway. She called George into her office.

Sam removed his coat and headed for the cloakroom. He waved his arm out of the door, asking for my coat.

I took it off and handed it to him.

'You had better make sure I get back to my room safely,' his muffled voice called out.

I smiled at him when he came out and headed off up the stairs.

'I've had a grand day, Mackenzie. Never wished to be teeny tiny before.'

I laughed and followed him into his room.

'Will you stay awhile?' he asked softly.

I shrugged and joined him on the bed.

'I've got something to show you that you might like,' he said, reaching for a computerised reading device that was on the bedside cabinet.

I leaned in closer as the screen lit up. He started tapping at the screen. I laughed when I saw what came up.

'Tom Thumb?'

'Teeny tiny,' he chuckled.

'Who put that in there?'

He laughed. 'Claire. She gave this to me before she left. There are loads of children's stories in here. I think she was slightly obsessed.'

'Are you going to read to me?'

'Yeah, why not.'

I found myself snuggling down into his fluffy pillow and once again feeling comforted in his warm presence.

The next thing I knew, George was shaking my shoulder.

'Mac, wake up. Wake up. It's time to go.'

I stirred, opened my eyes, and realised I had fallen asleep. I was so good at falling asleep. I could do it within the drop of a hat. My mum always said I was lucky. It took her a good couple of hours to feel tired and at least three chapters of a crime novel.

I sat up and looked sleepily at George.

He shook his head in disbelief. 'You're lucky Victoria didn't find you.'

I followed his eyes over to a sleeping Sam at my side.

'Come on,' he whispered. 'Let's go home.'

I got up and stretched. 'I fell asleep.'

George nodded. 'Yes, that's been established.'

I followed him out of the room and watched him close Sam's door.

'I didn't mean to,' I added.

‘Good thing you didn’t have to work at the pub tonight,’ said George, walking away towards the stairs. ‘Your shift would have ended by now.’

I clicked my neck from side to side.

‘What time is it?’ I asked.

George glanced at his watch. ‘Gone nine. I’ve been filling out Sam’s report. You can fill in the gaps tomorrow.’

I followed him down the stairs. ‘Nine?’

He stopped on the step below me. ‘You didn’t have work tonight, did you, or any other plans?’

I shook my weary head. ‘No.’ Then, it hit me. I froze on the stairway and gasped. ‘Oh crap, George. Salad!’

18

Malorie's big black jeep was parked in the driveway, indicating that she was home. There was no way I was going to knock on the door. I rushed inside my own house and practically flew up the stairs to my room. I went straight over to the window and slid the bottom half up.

Adam's window was closed and the blind was blocking me out.

I glanced over at my alarm clock to see the time. It was almost ten. George's faffing about with coats and paperwork had slowed us down, that and the light snow that started to fall again. He was a careful driver. One drop of rain would cause him to roll along at 20mph.

I checked my phone to see if I had any messages from Adam.

Nothing.

I looked back at his window. I could sense his disappointment in me. I felt equally disappointed.

I wasn't remotely hungry, due to the hotdog I had for my dinner at six. The onions were still repeating on me. However, I would have still eaten anything he made for me. I just had the feeling that my salad was in the bin.

I needed to talk to Adam. I wanted to explain. He had a right to know that I fell asleep on Sam's bed.

'Oh God, I can't tell him that.'

I knew I had to. I would want to know if the shoe were on the other foot. I made the executive decision to come clean there and then. It couldn't wait till morning.

'Don't tell him, Mac. It won't go down well at all. No, I must tell him. Don't do it. Oh, shut up.'

I had to stop talking to my room and get on with the distasteful job at hand.

I reached down and picked up a handful of grit and chucked it at his window. I cringed because it sounded extra loud. I quickly sat down on the window chair. That's what I called the green wooden seat that had been there for as long as I could remember.

I waited.

Nothing.

Ten minutes later, and I was still staring over at Adam's dark window. It was staring back at me, telling me to get stuffed.

I got up and went to the bathroom to brush my teeth. When I got back, I looked out the window. All I could see was falling snow.

I left my window open. I no longer cared about the chill. I noticed my phone on the floor and sat down in front of it. It was time to send Adam a text.

I began typing away and picked up quite a speed. The text turned into an essay all about my day and night and how sorry I was that I was a no-show. I probably explained way more than was actually needed for a text, but I was on a roll, and it was all coming out whether I liked it or not. Adam was getting the truth, the whole truth, and nothing but the truth. I ended the message telling him I still wanted my salad.

Ten minutes later. Nothing.

I sighed heavily and got up to sit on the bed. I reached over towards my pillows for my pyjamas. They were a navy-and-white stripy shirt and bottoms set, which suited my dad more than me, but I loved them. The fleece was soft and comfy, just perfect for a snowy night in Norfolk.

I was struggling to get the top over my head, because I was being lazy about unbuttoning it, when I felt a thump on my bed. I glanced down to see a chunk of cucumber sitting there. I turned sharply when I heard Adam's voice.

'I wish you would close your curtains when you're getting changed.'

I jumped and tugged the shirt down over my breasts. Wasn't quite sure how much flesh he had seen. I tried not to blush, but I could feel my cheeks burning already. I knew I could blame it on the cold air.

I rolled over my mattress and quickly landed in my window chair.

'Did you read my message?' I asked.

He was staring at me. I couldn't read his expression because it was snow-filled.

'Are you going to tell me about Sam?' he asked. He sounded just as cold as the snow settling on the ground between us.

'You know I can't talk about him properly because he's from work.'

'Are you allowed to sleep with the patients?' he asked sharply.

I twisted my lips. I knew all I could do was tell the truth. 'I didn't sleep with him. I fell asleep while he was reading to me on his bed.'

I no longer saw the snow. I saw my relationship with one of my closest friends blow away in the wind.

This is what happens when you kiss your friends. It complicates everything. Now I didn't have a friend or the chance of having a boyfriend. Adam was completely gone from my life the moment I had finished my sentence.

Adam was silent for quite some time.

All I wanted was to curl up with a hot water bottle in my bed and go to sleep.

'I'm sorry, Adds,' I called over, knowing I had to say something before he slammed his window shut on me forever.

'So am I, Mac,' he said softly.

I waited until I was sure he wouldn't open his window to me again, and then I closed mine slightly and climbed into bed. I turned off my lamp and looked over at the window to watch the falling snowflakes that were just visible, thanks to a street light that shone between our houses. I felt something under my elbow. It was the piece of cucumber he had thrown at me. I picked it up and twiddled it in my fingers, and then I ate it.

* * *

'How did salad-gate go?' asked George.

I climbed inside his car. I started to cry. I didn't know I was going to cry. It just happened.

He cranked the heating up, removed his seatbelt, and leaned over to give me a hug.

'I always knew you liked Adam, but bloody hell, Mac, I wasn't expecting you to start crying over him already.'

I sniffed into George's pink jumper and lifted my head. 'What do you mean, you always knew I liked him?'

He reached forward to the glovebox, opened it, and pulled out a tissue for me.

I blew my nose and waited for his response.

George put on his seatbelt and started to drive. 'Well, Mac, it was obvious.'

I didn't know it was obvious because I didn't know it existed. I had only ever viewed Adam as a friend. I was sure of it. Wasn't I? George was messing with my memories. Adam and I were only friends until the other night. Maybe it did start before that. Is that even possible for me not to recognise our feelings for each other?

'I've got a headache, George.'

'We'll be at work soon. You can grab some painkillers there.'

I looked down at the scrunched tissue in my hand. 'I don't think we were love interests to each other until recently.'

George smiled widely. It was a goofy grin. The one he reserved for telling me that he knew something I didn't know.

I wasn't biting.

I bit.

'What, George? What are you grinning about?'

'How blind you can be to the world, Mac. Adam was in love with you in school. You spend so much time with each other, and he's the one you turn to whenever you feel down and need support.'

I cut in, 'That's not true, George. I come to you too.'

He shrugged. 'You've kissed now. That doesn't come about from thin air. That's been building for a long time. Way too long, in my opinion.'

I glanced at him as he glanced at me.

'Doesn't matter now,' I said quietly. 'He hates me. I told him I fell asleep on Sam's bed while Sam was reading to me.'

George had his serious face on. 'Hope you haven't told him much about Sam.'

I shook my head. 'Of course not. I just had to mention his name while telling the truth.'

'I can see why it didn't go down well.'

I grumbled under my breath.

'I need you to be careful with Sam,' said George.

'What do you mean?'

'That whole empath thing you have about you. You bond too quickly to broken people. You can't do that working at Moreton Hall.'

'I do feel quite bonded to Sam.'

George nodded. 'Yeah, I noticed.'

There was a long silence between us.

George had something on his mind, which became apparent when he blurted out, 'Do you love Adam?'

I went to speak, but he quickly added, 'Not like you love me. You know what I mean.'

'Everything is easy with him. Everything feels right when I'm with Adam. Oh God, have I always loved him?'

George nodded.

'Well, it doesn't matter now. He hates me,' I said, feeling sorry for myself. 'Plus, he's going on some arty tour in the spring, so I won't see him for a long time, not that he's going to see me anytime soon. He's blocked me out. There wasn't even anything in the window this morning.'

'He'll come around, Mac. Give him time to process you on another man's bed.'

I raised my eyebrows. 'Is that your professional advice?'

George laughed.

'How's your pen pal situation anyway?'

'Don't change the subject.' He paused. 'It's going all right, as it happens.'

At least someone's love life was uncomplicated. I thought I could resort to writing to Adam. He wouldn't know the letter was from me. He'd open it, and then he'd see my name and probably screw it up and throw it in his robot-looking bin that I saw under his desk. What kind of bedroom is that anyway? All contemporary and fingerprint-less. Someone could have an operation in that room.

I remembered when Adam had his first operation after his accident. We all thought he would be able to walk again. We wished so hard for that.

I looked out at the settled snow on the fields around us. It was clean and crisp. So beautiful, like a huge white carpet. I felt grateful for being snug in George's warm car, and for the fact that I didn't leave any marks on Malorie's stair carpet. That carpet was haunting me.

'Probably going to be a bit bumpy at work today, Mac.'

I turned to George. 'Oh, why's that?'

'Sam had a good day yesterday.'

I shrugged. 'So?'

'He probably won't have one today.'

'What makes you think that?'

'Guilt,' said George flatly. 'He'll feel overwhelmed with guilt today.'

'You sure?'

'You can never be sure, Mac.'

* * *

George's hunch was spot on. Sam refused breakfast, any tea offered, and he didn't have his shower at eleven, or at any other time.

Victoria had put him on amber watch, which basically meant we all had to keep an eye on him, and I wasn't allowed to make small talk, or any talk. I was specifically told.

I spent a couple of hours before lunch sitting in the office filling out my report on Sam's day trip. I had no idea how to write out a report, but George said I had to fill in the gaps, so there I was filling in gaps that didn't include Sam holding my face. I felt like I was betraying him. I didn't want to put our day on display for all the psych doctors to read. Some things felt private.

It was when Sam didn't come down to lunch that I decided to go against Victoria's orders and do what I thought was best.

I took a tray up to Sam's room. There wasn't much on the plate, just some hard-boiled egg sandwiches, a pork pie, and a handful of salt and vinegar crisps. There was also a small glass of orange juice, as I knew that was his favourite drink.

I knocked on the door. Waited. Pressed my ear up against the wood. Listened. Knocked again. Waited. And that was enough of that. I let myself in.

The room was dark. The curtains were still closed. Sam was pretty much hiding under the bed covers. I could just about make out the hair on the top of his head.

I knew how he felt, sort of. I'd had days like that too at times. You just want to disappear for a while. Forget the world exists, and try again another day.

I plonked the tray down on top of the chest of drawers. The noise made him grumble. I went over to the brown curtains and pulled them apart, then opened the window. The fresh winter air hit me straight in the face. I tried not to cough. I smiled at the snow and ignored Sam's muffled complaints. It was time to get up and take on the world, or in Sam's case, just get up.

Sam flipped his duvet over in agitation. His head swiftly lifted to glare at the light coming in from the window. He didn't look one bit happy.

'What are you doing, Mackenzie?' he snapped.

'I brought you lunch,' I replied. I kept my tone as light and soft as the fallen snow, but it didn't help.

Sam flopped back down and pulled his covers over his head. 'I'm not hungry.'

I reached forward and yanked his quilt down a bit.

He shot up and pulled it back towards him. 'What do you think you're doing?'

'Getting you out of bed. It's gone lunchtime. You haven't eaten all day, and you're missing the snow scene outside. We could do snow angels.'

'Snow angels?'

I shrugged and sat down at the foot of his bed. 'It will be fun.' I watched him grimace.

'I don't want to have fun, Mackenzie. Can you just go away?'

I shook my head. 'Nope.'

'Mackenzie, it's not a good time, okay.'

'I know it's not. That's why you have to get up.'

'Why?' he snapped. 'What will that achieve? Will it improve my health, or wipe away the past? Will I suddenly feel like a normal person? Will everything be grand?'

I really had no idea. I just knew that hiding under the covers never made the demons disappear.

Sam fell back to his bed and tucked himself away again, so I climbed over him and got into bed alongside him.

'Mackenzie, what are you doing?' his muffled voice asked from beneath the duvet.

'If you're going to stay here all day, so am I.'

Sam flipped the cover over so that both our heads were showing. He glanced sideways at me and wrinkled his brow. His stern expression had softened a touch. He sat up a bit and placed his arms outside of the quilt.

I mimicked his actions.

He sighed deeply. 'What do you want from me, Mackenzie?' he asked quietly, as though deflated.

'I just want you to heal.'

'Why don't you try healing your own life.'

I frowned. 'Who says my life needs healing?'

He shrugged. 'It needs something. I mean, look at you.' He cast a significant look my way.

He was starting to get on my nerves. 'What's that supposed to mean?'

'Don't you think you should start getting a life? You swan around here like there's nothing else in the world to be getting on with. Life's short, Mackenzie. Go and take some chances.'

I wanted to say that I did take chances, but I rarely did. I didn't get a chance to say anything because he hadn't finished.

'Have you even got any wants or wishes? What about a person? Do you even have that?'

'I have an Adam,' I snapped.

He raised his eyebrows. 'An Adam?'

I sank slightly. 'I'm not too sure what we are.'

He sniffed and turned to face me. 'What's he like?'

I didn't need much time to think about it. 'He's like your favourite slippers that you never want to throw away.'

A muffled laugh came from him. 'Slippers.'

I shrugged. 'I don't know. He's just Adam.'

'How long have you known him?'

'Pretty much all my life.'

'And you still don't know where you stand with him?'

I was starting to resent the way Sam was sounding. George often spoke to me the same way. Anyone would think they were the experts on love and relationships.

Sam huffed. 'I bet you haven't even been truthful with him about how you feel.'

I frowned. 'Some conversations are tricky.'

He didn't seem too bothered by my words. 'I think you're being lazy about it, if I'm honest.'

'What would you know?'

'I know that you left school at eighteen and went on to do little else with your life. I know that you obviously have feelings for some lad, but your faffing around is causing it to slip away just like the rest of your future.'

'Oh, well, just say what you really think.'

He raised one shoulder up to his cheek. 'If I had my time over, I would make the most of every day.'

I had to laugh. 'Your time over. What are you, ninety?'

His face was serious. 'My life is over now, Mackenzie. That's it for me.'

I touched his hand. 'No, it's not. You just need to heal.'

He started to play with my fingers. 'I don't think I ever will.'

My heart sank at the empty emotion in his voice. He was so sad.

'Perhaps you can accept your life for what it is now and simply adjust to that, rather than trying to become whole again,' I said gently.

He nodded and breathed out a long sigh. 'All my life, I've tried to adapt to my circumstances. Hasn't really got me anywhere. Not too bothered about trying anything anymore, if I'm to be honest about that.'

'You were happy once. It's possible for you to be happy again.'

'The only time I truly felt happy was when I was a part of Mindforder.'

'Even though they beat you up?'

He removed his hand from mine. 'I broke the rules. I took my punishment.'

I could barely register his words. Was he actually defending their cruelty?

'Do you wish you were back there?' I had to ask. I wanted to know if there was any chance he would return to them once freed of Moreton Hall.

He shook his head. 'No,' he said simply.

I wasn't sure if I was entering uncharted waters. This was George's job. I was just the general dogsbody. Should I be asking him to delve? It wasn't like me to spend so much time thinking it through. Sam made me think about a lot of things. It was as though he had a magical way of slowing down my brain.

'Why did you leave Mindforder?'

He looked at me, eyes wide with curiosity. 'Doesn't it say in my file?'

'There's not a lot in your file. You won't tell anyone all the nitty gritty.'

His mouth curled slightly. 'Nitty gritty, you say?'

I shrugged. 'Probably not the best choice of words.'

He shook his head and scrunched his nose. 'Probably not, but then you wouldn't be you if you chose your words wisely, would you?'

'I guess I'm just a bit confused.'

He laughed. 'You're confused! You should try joining a cult.'

I gave him a sympathetic smile. 'You seemed to enjoy a lot about Mindforder, but you walked away.'

He scratched the side of his face. His eyes narrowed as he cleared the back of his throat. 'I didn't walk away. I escaped. We escaped.'

I didn't mean to make light of it, but he sounded so dramatic, so I blurted out that fact along with a scoff.

His eyes darted my way. 'Our lives were in danger.'

Danger is a serious word. I wasn't about to make light of that. 'I know your life is in danger still, but I don't know why. What did you do to them?'

He raised his hands slightly from the bed. 'Found out the truth about the Island.'

This was starting to get cryptic. I lacked the patience for half-truths and unfinished stories. Every part of me was urging Sam to just spit it out. What was his backstory? Fill in the missing pages. Tell me. Tell George. Tell Victoria. Tell someone the full story.

'What truth was that?'

'It wasn't Bluebird who ran Mindforder. It was Buddy, and he had his own agenda, but there's nothing anyone can do about it. No one would ever believe me. He's way too powerful to ever bring down. There are millions of members of Mindforder, and they all idolise the man. That's why when I leave here, I'll be sent off somewhere remote with a new identity so that his people never find me. I'm a loose end, you see.'

I had never felt scared working at Moreton Hall before. I had never felt scared for someone else since Adam had his accident. I felt scared, really scared. It must have flashed across my face because Sam reached out and held my hand.

'It's all right, you know, Mackenzie. They won't find me.'

I squeezed his hand. 'I hope they don't, Sam. I really hope they don't.'

He lifted my hand and kissed the back of it while it was tightly clenched inside his.

My eyes glazed over as they met with his gentle face. He was so lovely. He had kindness written all over him. He did not deserve the life he was living.

He smiled warmly. 'Shall we just go back to sleep now, and call it a day?'

I ignored his attempt to shrug off the darkness.

'Not until you tell me the story about Buddy,' I insisted.

'It's not a nice story. He's an evil man.'

'How did you find that out?'

'It wasn't me. It was Maggie. She was the one who discovered what was going on.'

He had my full attention. 'What happened?'

'It was the night I got my scars.'

19

Maggie

I walked as far as the back of the medical supplies hut and I had to sit down. I felt sick from transporting Sam to the Ward. I didn't want to go home anyway. I knew what was waiting for me there. Nothing.

I hid myself in among the trees and tried to ground myself. The sun was gone, but the air was still warm and adding to my dazed state of mind. Nothing felt real.

Three days, I remembered. I have to go back in three days. What was I supposed to do for three days? Go to work? Act normal? What were the rules regarding life after a whipping?

I glanced down at my weary legs. They had died and left me. I reached forward and started to rub some life back into them.

'Ouch!' The splinters in my hands said hello. I could see some of the bigger ones. I winced pulling them out. I stopped when I heard voices. I turned my head slightly to take a peek.

Outside a small hut beside the medical supply hut were two men struggling with a large package that was wrapped in bin bags. I tilted my head a touch and narrowed my eyes. What they were carrying looked suspiciously like a dead body.

I told myself it couldn't be.

I watched them load the item into the back of a military truck.

They both went back inside the hut. I took a chance and scrambled closer. I wasn't thinking about anything. I just wanted to see if the bin bags really were concealing a body, or if somebody had drugged me and my imagination was running wild, because I was having the most surreal day of my life.

I froze behind a tree as the two men came back out. My right eye scanned the scene. They were the men who usually stood behind Guide Claris. The left and the right Guardians. Eliza's ex-husband and his partner in crime.

Was it a crime?

They were complaining to each other about each other. I knew no one else was around because they weren't allowed to speak. They obviously felt secure enough to disobey the rules.

I waited for them to go away again, but they didn't go anywhere except around to the front of the truck, where they climbed in ready to drive off.

I sprinted forward as the truck's engine rattled the vehicle, and I jumped inside the back. I pulled the canvas flap back down behind me and turned to the package on the floor.

It was definitely shaped like a body.

I, again, told myself it couldn't be.

I carefully manoeuvred myself over towards the head-shaped part. I was on my knees and could feel the hard floor digging in my bones. I leaned over to smell the bin bags. A cold chemical hit my nostrils. I hovered one hand over the head. There was definitely a cool feel coming from beneath the plastic. Using my sore fingertips, I carefully started to unravel the cover, piece by piece. I didn't want to tear it in any way. A loose piece flapped open, so I used that as my leverage.

Slowly and steadily, in among the bumpy ride, I removed the black bags until there wasn't anything else left to move. My hand shot up to cover my mouth as I came face to face with a dead man.

I tried so hard not to cry, scream, yell out, or make any noise. My head felt light from me practically holding my breath. I could feel my lip trembling and see the tears blurring my vision. I managed to control the air escaping through my blood-stained fingers. I took a moment to steady my nerves and focus.

My exhausted brain went into overdrive. What was happening? Why was this happening? When did this happen? What was this place?

I knew I had to get off the truck before being discovered, else I would end up in the freezer.

I quietly kissed my shaky fingertips and placed them down upon Tom's icy forehead.

It seemed wrong to mummify his face in rubbish bags, but I had no choice. I covered him back up.

The truck was going at a steady pace over wide, gravel pathways. That's all I could see when I peered out of the canvas flap at the back. There were trees either side and emptiness behind us. I had no idea where I was, or how far we had gone. It was dark and quiet. There wasn't even any noise coming from Left and Right sitting up front. The sound of the engine filled the void. Even my heartbeat had faded.

I gazed down at the road. I had to jump while the truck was moving. It was the only way. I knew it was going to hurt, but not as much as getting caught.

The truck started to slow. An opportunity. My legs were hanging off the back, shaking. My body shifted sideways as we turned a corner. I leapt forward towards the grassy verge, in hope that it would soften the blow. It didn't. My knees scraped the gravel, and my arms were scratched by twigs and stones. Something in my lower back twinged, but I had managed to somehow save my head.

I stayed still, curled up in the foetal position for a minute or two, catching my breath and silently saying my thanks.

Trying not to groan, I sat up to see if anyone had seen me. There was silence and darkness. Even the trees didn't rustle. Then, I heard some distant mumbling.

I shot up and scrambled closer to the pathway to look in the direction the truck went. There was light up ahead. I squinted my eyes, trying to make out what it was.

Keeping to the edge, close to the woods, I made my way towards the light. My legs hurt, but I ignored them along with the blood dripping from my knees.

I had made the plan to say I had become disorientated once I left the Ward and had wandered into the unknown. There wasn't anyone to lie to yet, but the lie was ready and in place. I certainly looked like a disorientated person. I could be believable, if my life depended on it. I didn't want to be beaten like Sam, or dead like Tom.

Now wasn't the time to think about Sam, or Tom, or getting caught. Now was about finding out where I was, and how I was going to get home, and what that light was.

As I neared the light, I saw the truck again. It was stationary and abandoned. The light shining above it came from a streetlamp. I hadn't seen one of those since I lived in the village. We had to carry lanterns if we wanted to walk about in the dark.

I avoided the light by keeping to the trees. I reached the front of the truck to see a gateway. It was made of metal railings and was way taller than me. I crept around the side of the wall it was attached to and made my way along the brickwork. The forest had grown up to the wall and in some parts entwined itself. I tugged at my dress a couple of times when it got caught in the foliage. I had given up on counting the cuts and bruises my walk in the woods had given me.

When I felt I was at a safe enough distance from the metal gate, I used fallen logs to elevate myself up so I could peer over the wall.

There was a detached beige house sitting in the middle of another woodland patch. It looked like a child had drawn it, with its four windows and front door. A child would add flowers and place the sun in the top corner of the page. This house looked lost and alone and in need of some love.

I pondered over its purpose.

I looked around for any signs of security. There was light in every window of the house, but no other signs of life. Even Left and Right had disappeared. No doubt, with Tom's body.

If there was ever a time to not do something stupid, it was now, but I was far too frazzled to listen to my intuition. I climbed over the wall while wondering how long I had been away from home. How long was I in that truck? How long did I stay with Tom? How long did it take me to get up the nerve to jump out of a moving vehicle?

The whole night seemed to be moving in slow motion. I hadn't just lost track of time, I had lost track of my mind.

I kept my eyes glued to the windows as I ran across the grass to face the back of the house. There were more windows around that side than the front, and there was an extension shaped like a sandcastle.

There was a small green shed nearby. I hid along its side. I could almost smell the rust peeling off its worn metal walls.

Someone moved across the top left window. Their shadow forced me back into mine.

I peered up, focused on the light, not quite sure what I was doing.

There it was again. A person. Someone stood at the window, staring out. They didn't move from their spot for what seemed like forever but was probably only a minute.

Suddenly, my vision cleared. I could make out the face in the window. It was Beatrix. I almost leapt forward, I was so pleased to see her.

My brain felt foggy, half asleep. I couldn't think straight. I didn't know what to do for the best. My arm seemed to take over. I waved up at the window.

Beatrix was staring forward not down. She still hadn't moved an inch.

I stepped forward, revealing myself to the house. I quickly ran towards the brickwork, away from any downstairs windows. I grabbed some dirt from the ground, ran away from the wall, tossed it up towards Beatrix, and then ran back to hide against the wall.

I knew from my position that even if she looked down, she wouldn't be able to see me. I would have to move away from the house. I did a quick sprint over to the shed and quickly turned to see if anyone was looking.

Beatrix was.

I waved.

She moved.

I watched her open her window, but it only lifted up about five inches. I could see her dipping down to place her mouth between the gap. Her hand wriggled through and started pointing at something.

Me? No. The shed? No. The other side of the shed.

I couldn't get around the back of the rust bucket. The forest had sculpted itself around its back wall. I had no choice. I revealed myself to the house again as I made my way around the front of the shed to see what was on the other side.

She had to be kidding me.

My eyes dropped to the bottom of the long metal ladder. I told myself that I was not climbing a ladder up to the top of a house but found myself doing exactly that.

Every single part of my body had taken on a life of its own, because if I owned it, it would not have done what it was doing. In fact, I'd be tucked up in bed right now, crying over Sam. But, no. I was suddenly at the top of a ladder.

'Beatrix,' I whispered through the gap in the window. 'What is this place? What are you doing here?' I had many questions, but they were the only ones to escape my cloudy mind.

Beatrix reached her hand through and grabbed a hold of mine. Her face was pale and afraid. Her sleeve was torn, and her hair looked unwashed and ratty. I'd never seen her looking like that before. She was always well turned out, and her face was always fresh and cheerful.

'Maggie,' she whispered, her voice cracked and sore. 'You shouldn't be here.'

'What's happening, Beatrix?' I went to glance down to see if anyone was there, but the part of my brain that knew I didn't like heights thought better of it.

Beatrix tightened her hold on my fingers. 'You have to get out of here before somebody sees you.'

I had kind of guessed that part already.

'Get off the Island,' she warned.

'What's going on?'

She glanced over her shoulder, then back at me. 'Maggie, it's not what we thought. It's all a lie.'

I felt the full rush of fear sweep through my body. At least I knew I was still functioning because, after my night, I was starting to question my sanity. I felt trapped in a nightmare. I longed to wake up. Wake up next to Sam. My hand shook.

'It's Buddy, Maggie,' she whispered, tugging at my fingers. 'He's a fake.'

'What are you talking about?'

'He brings us here before taking us to the Main House. He explains the new rules.'

'What new rules?'

She took a shaky breath and loosened her grip on my hand. 'He is in charge around here, not Bluebird. He is the one making all the babies up at the Main House. There are no chosen ones, just us and him.'

I knew I had to remain focused. I could hear the words coming out of her mouth, and I could see the fear in her eyes, but I couldn't quite grasp everything I was being told. It didn't make sense. None of it made any sense. Buddy was a hero to us. He wouldn't treat women that way. He was Bluebird's faithful servant. He was loyal to her, and Mindforder. He was everything.

I shook my head at her. 'No, Beatrix. You must be mistaken.'

She squeezed my hand. 'Please, Maggie. Believe me. You must escape this place because they will never let you leave, and one day you will be here, in this house, with him.'

She looked queasy.

'Beatrix, are you all right?'

The tears had filled her eyes. She shook her head. 'Please, go.'

There was no way I was leaving her.

She pushed my hand away. 'Find a way to escape. Tell no one, especially the men. They cannot be trusted. You can't trust anyone. You must be careful.'

I didn't know whether or not to tell her about Tom? Did she already know? Did she think he left her here?

'I'm not leaving you, Beatrix.'

'You have no choice. I'm locked in, and this window does not open any more than this.' She paused, listening. She looked back into my eyes. 'Maggie, if they find you, they will kill you. Do you understand?'

I felt I was starting to.

'Maggie, you can't help me right now, but you can help you,' she whispered. 'On the west side of the Island, towards the hills, there is a tight ledge that leads you around to a small beach. No one goes there. There are trees you can use to make a raft. Go there in your spare time. Make sure you are not followed. Build your raft, Maggie. Build it and sail away.'

I couldn't believe what was happening. It was a nightmare. So surreal. One big fat surreal nightmare that I knew wouldn't disappear.

It was like she could read my mind. 'I know this sounds crazy, Maggie, but it's all true. Don't let him do to you what he has been doing to me here. Don't let him take you to the Main House. Escape.'

'I don't know how to make a raft. I don't even know where we are, let alone sail off somewhere.'

'You have no choice. You do not want this for your life.'

I watched a tear roll down her lifeless cheek.

'Maggie,' she said softly, 'I need you to escape and tell the world what is happening here. You're my only hope of freedom.'

I pushed on the window. 'We can go together. I just need to get this window open.'

Her hand reached out and grabbed mine. 'Stop.'

'No, I can do this,' I said, frantically clawing the wooden framework with my free hand.

She jolted me. 'Maggie, stop.'

I wanted to cry, to scream, to hit something, someone.

'Please, go,' she whispered. 'Please, Maggie. I'm begging you. Escape, and tell the world.'

I couldn't leave without telling her. I just couldn't. 'Tom…'

She cut me off, 'They killed him. He was given a choice to go back to a village or become a Guardian. He chose to leave. You see, Maggie. No one leaves. They can't afford for anyone to leave. The people who really run Mindforder don't want anyone to ever find out the truth.'

'I'm finding it hard to take in the truth.'

Her scared face turned angry and serious. 'I've been told that Bluebird is locked away somewhere in the Main House. That's the real reason no one sees her anymore. He has done that to her.'

Life flowed through my body. My blood pressure rose along with a sickness in my stomach. I could feel heat in my face and tightness in my chest.

Beatrix nodded. 'Save us all, Maggie.'

I knew I couldn't be the hero of the hour. Not me. Not scrawny, pathetic me, who couldn't fight her way out of a paper bag. Not me, who let people walk all over her for her entire life. Not me, who couldn't even save Sam. How was I expected to do this task? To bring down a religion followed by millions. To save women from a powerful sociopath. Build a bloody raft!

Beatrix gently pushed my hand. 'Go, Maggie. Go now. I'll be all right knowing you are out there finding a way to free us.'

I shook my head. 'I don't know how long it will take.'

She smiled. It was weak but filled with meaning. 'I'm not expecting an overnight miracle.'

I pulled her hand to my mouth and kissed the tips of her fingers.

‘I’ll never stop trying,’ I promised.

‘I’ll never stop believing in you.’

I didn’t want to leave her. She knew that, but she made me go. She closed the window on me and turned her back.

I had a job to do.

I really wanted Sam.

I don’t know how I managed to climb down the ladder without throwing up, but I did, and I put it back in place beside the shed without making any noise.

Beatrix waved to me. One slight hand gesture wishing me good luck. I needed more than luck. I needed help. I needed to find my way back home.

I made my way back across the grounds and over the same wall I had entered by. I retraced my steps, to the best of my dark forest knowledge, and stopped just short of the roadside.

I figured if I followed the road, it was bound to lead me some of the way, or at least lead to somewhere I might recognise.

I stayed hidden in amongst the trees as I walked in the only direction I could think of.

I don’t know how long I was walking for when I remembered what Sam had told me about the stars. It wasn’t that long ago he was pointing at the sky and telling me which direction the stars were at during certain times of the year. I must admit, I didn’t take in everything he said. Plus, neither of us knew which hemisphere we were in, but recently, there had been a big bright star straight ahead of our front door.

I started to head towards the brightest star I could see. I prayed it would guide me home.

I almost laughed when I saw the back of the Kitchen. People really could navigate their way by stars. I just followed one bright one, with full on scepticism and little to no hope.

It wasn't until I slid down the back of my closed and locked hut door that I felt the reality hit. My legs huddled into my chest, and my tears soaked into my ripped, muddy, bloodstained dress.

20

I woke on the floor the next morning, slumped by the front door. Every fibre of my being ached. My throat was dry, and my eyes just as sore as my limbs. I sat up slowly and noticed my hands. They were cut to shreds, filled with splinters, and covered in dried blood. Sam's blood. I glanced down at my lap. More blood. I rubbed my eyes and pulled away when a splinter in the side of my hand scratched my right eye. Struggling with the back of my dress, I stood up and pulled it off, over my head.

I looked down at my bruised and battered body. My knees were grazed, and there were streaky lines of dried blood down my shins.

I limped to the fridge to get some cold water. My head felt light, and my body weak. I saw the milk and drank that instead. The whole jug. Down in one.

I looked myself over again. I knew I had to clean up. I just felt too numb to move, but I did. I made my way into the bathroom.

The face staring back at me in the small mirror was a new face. One I hadn't been introduced to before. I'd seen many of my faces over the years, but this one, this one was definitely new.

I glanced down at the sink and placed my hands in the bowl. I could see them trembling slightly. I hadn't noticed until I looked. I ran the taps and started to pull out as many splinters I could see. It really hurt.

My mind drifted back to Sam's beating. My hands had no right to hurt. My body had no right to feel pain.

Blood faded as it diluted and swirled down the plughole.

I slowly walked over to the shower. I listened to the trickling water as I removed my underwear. The noise used to soothe me. Now it was stinging me and washing away the night before, but not the nightmare.

* * *

I didn't know what time it was, but I had eaten, washed my dress out, and had fallen asleep on the bed, when someone knocked on the door. I answered it, half-awake, wearing one of Sam's tee-shirts and a pair of knickers.

Annie's eyes widened. She hurried herself inside and quickly closed the door.

'What are you wearing?' she whispered. I think her husband was outside. 'Do you know how much trouble you would be in if someone else saw you dressed like that?' She didn't comment on the cuts and bruises on my arms and legs.

Everything hurt, so I made my way over to the table and sat down on one of the chairs. The one Sam usually sat on.

'What do you want, Annie?' I asked, sounding slightly cold but not meaning to.

She sat opposite me. Her hands rested on the table. 'I came here to see if you were okay today.'

My eyes sarcastically rolled up to glare into hers.

'Yeah, I know. It's a dumb question,' she said. 'But what else can I say?'

Nothing, I thought, just leave.

I shrugged. Even that hurt.

'Is there anything I can do?' she asked.

I had many things I wanted to say. Save Beatrix. Help Sam. Free Bluebird. Call the police.

I shook my head.

Annie glanced around my house. 'Your husband will be home soon. Take this time to get the house straight, pick up what bits and pieces you need from supplies, and just rest in between. Neither of you will be expected to work for a week.'

One whole week off. Wow! It actually amused me.

I nodded.

Annie made for the door. I didn't get up. She smiled softly and left. I looked around my neat and tidy home. There wasn't anything to get straight, except Mindforder.

* * *

I had sat around indoors doing little else but stare at walls, feeling numb, lost, and alone. The hut was clean. Clothes were hanging in the wardrobe, waiting for Sam. The food situation was bleak, but I planned to pick up some bread and milk on the way to the Ward.

It was the first day I had got dressed out of the time I had spent alone. Sam's green tee-shirt was the only other item sitting in the laundry basket with my underwear. I had forced myself out of its comfy hold. It smelled like him. It was all I had. I slept in it and snuggled my face into the sleeves every night, pretending he was by my side. Tonight, he would be.

I looked glumly around the house before taking the key out of the door. I didn't want to go outside. I wasn't in the mood to see people, let alone talk to them. I had no idea who was fake, who was innocent, or who was vulnerable.

Sam was waiting for me to collect him. It was time. It was my duty.

My sore eyes squinted as the sun blared down on me. I tugged my hat down and tipped my head and kept it that way all the way to the Larder. I got some bread and milk and was glad to get out of there without seeing anyone who would stop to talk to me.

There were two women there, in the cold section, but they just stared, and then, no doubt, gossiped about me.

I just watched my feet taking one step at a time. They led me all the way to the Ward, where the nurse met me at the door and told me to wait outside.

Sitting on the steps, I twiddled with the handle on my cloth shopping bag. My mind was focused on the sun burning into my shoes, melting my feet.

Birds sang sweetly nearby, and a gentle breeze blew my tied-back hair, waking me ever so slightly from my fixed trance.

'Maggie.'

I heard his soft voice behind me.

I turned quickly and stood up to see him for the first time since I had brought him there. He was wearing clean beige trousers and no top. I felt my face move by itself, trying to smile. My heart was smiling, but I could feel little else about myself.

Sam's face lacked emotion. He just looked tired.

'The nurse would like to speak to you,' he told me.

I picked up my bag and walked inside to the desk. The sterile smell and cool air filled my nostrils, making me sniff.

The nurse had about as much emotion in his face as Sam. He shuffled a piece of paper towards me along with a small paper bag.

'You need to sign here,' he pointed out, 'and here.'

I took the pen and signed my name.

Angel Maggie

The nurse glanced up at me and gave a slight nod. 'The rest of his antibiotics are in that bag. Make sure he finishes the course.'

I nodded and took the medicine and placed it in my shopping bag.

'I need to see him again in four days,' said the nurse, looking back at his desk.

'I'll bring him,' I said quietly.

'Don't get his back wet,' he added. 'You can wash around the stitches, but they must stay dry.'

'Okay.'

I glanced down the end of the hut to see if Ross was still inside. All of the beds were empty. The nurse caught my attention.

'He won't be expected to work, so stay home, and stay clean.'

I felt insulted about the clean comment. We were always clean. I gave him a slight nod, hoping that would be all.

He nodded back and walked away.

I turned and headed outside. I froze on seeing Sam's back. I felt tears hit my eyes and a lump hit the back of my throat.

He sensed my presence and looked over his shoulder at me. The action forced me to roll back my tears and move my feet.

Standing at his side on the steps, we both looked towards some nearby trees. Neither of us seemed to be able to speak.

He glanced down at the shopping bag in my hand and gently transferred it over into his.

'Ready?' he asked.

I nodded and took a step towards home. I wanted to be by his side, but it was forbidden for him to walk next to me. I could feel him just behind me, slightly to my left. Every so often, I peered over my shoulder at him. His head was tilted towards the ground every time I looked. I realised that I should have brought his hat. I was annoyed with myself for being so thoughtless.

We passed by six people on our way home. Nobody spoke to us. They politely buried their heads and scurried away as quickly as they could. I wondered if they weren't allowed to speak to us anymore. Not that I cared. I just wanted to go home. Home to the village where I was happy. The only time I had ever been happy, until I met Sam, that is.

I opened the door to our home and waited for Sam to come inside before locking us in.

He removed his shoes and went straight to the kitchen to put away the shopping.

I took my shoes off and went straight to the bedroom to get out of my hot dress and into my indoor dress.

Sam was leaning over the sink, staring into the empty bowl, by the time I got back. He glanced over at me.

'There's not much here.' He gave a nod towards the fridge.

'I haven't needed much,' I said quietly.

He turned to face me fully. 'Have you been eating, Maggie?'

I shook my head. 'I haven't been very hungry.'

I watched the concern flash across his face. 'Are you hungry now?'

'No.'

'Could you manage tea and toast?' he asked, knowing I could always manage that.

I shook my head. 'Do you need to lie down, Sam?' I asked, pointing behind me into the bedroom. 'I made the bed.'

'I'm okay.'

I glanced over at the sofa. 'I was thinking I'd sleep out here until you're…' I didn't know what to say, 'healed.' It was the only word that came to mind. 'I'm worried I might accidently turn over in the night and knock your back.'

He glanced at the sofa, then at me. 'We'll risk it,' he told me flatly.

There was a long silence.

Neither of us moved.

I spoke first. 'How are you?'

He didn't get the chance to answer because the heavy weight of my tears couldn't sit in my eyes any longer.

'Oh, Maggie,' he whispered.

I angrily wiped my tears away quickly. They had no right showing themselves.

Sam rushed forward and cradled me into his arms, and for the first time in days, I felt safe.

I was mindful of his wounded back, so my hands only held the top of his arms.

'It's okay, Maggie,' he whispered into my hair.

'I'm sorry,' I cried.

He tilted himself back and placed his hands on my face. 'You have nothing to be sorry about.'

'What they did to you…'

'Is not your fault.'

'I, I didn't stop them.'

'You had no power there, Maggie. Neither of us did.'

I wished my eyes weren't so blurry. I wanted to be able to see him clearly. I missed seeing his gentle eyes. I missed his warm smile. I missed his arms around me.

'I missed you, Sam.'

He rested his forehead on mine. 'I missed you too, Maggie.'

I lifted my face and hoped he would kiss me.

He did.

When his lips left mine, I said, 'I want to go home.'

He took a step back and lowered his head. 'I understand,' he said quietly. 'But we can't just come here and have all the good. We have to take the rough with the smooth. I broke the rules. I took my punishment. We'll be okay now. Everything will go back to how it was. You don't have to worry.'

I couldn't let him think that way. Not anymore. He needed to know the truth about everything he believed in, about Beatrix, about Tom.

The worry hit me hard. I sat down at the kitchen table and rested my arms on my lap. I stared at the wood, and a hundred words ran through my mind all at once.

Beatrix told me not to tell anyone. Not to trust anyone, but I wanted to tell Sam. To trust him. What if I was wrong? What if he didn't believe me? How was I supposed to make a raft without him? How was I ever going to leave the Island without him?

Sam sat opposite me. He reached his hands across the table, beckoning for mine.

I held his hands and his gaze.

He looked remorseful. 'I'm so sorry I shamed you, Maggie. If I could take it back I would. I'd change it all. Ever since I got here, all I've done is mess everything up. I can't get anything right. I'm not a good husband. I'm not a good Guard. I'm useless.'

His broken words were tearing me apart inside. None of what he was saying made sense to me. To me, he was wonderful. He was everything.

I shook my head at him. 'You're not useless, Sam.'

Tears were in his eyes. His shoulders were hunched, and his face worn through. 'I've done everything wrong.'

I lowered my head until it was resting on his hands holding mine. I sighed deeply to myself. I felt too weary to cry anymore. Everything just felt quiet. As quiet and broken as Sam's voice.

Okay. It was time. No more tears. No more sadness. No more broken hearts. No more Buddy.

I sat up and released his hands.

He frowned at my stern expression. 'What is it, Maggie?'

'I need to tell you something. You're not going to like it, but if you truly do care for me, you will believe me.' I hoped.

'I'll believe you, Maggie.' He seemed genuine.

'I found something out while you were in the Ward.' I was quickly discovering that it wasn't as easy to say as I first thought.

Sam looked serious. He looked worried. 'Are we to stay married?' he asked.

'What? No. That's not it. Is that what you're worried about?'

He raised one shoulder to his cheek.

I got up and knelt down before him on my sore knees. I winced, and he noticed. I tipped myself to sit sideways.

'We'll always be married, Sam, no matter what,' I assured him, while trying not to show any pain.

Sam wasn't listening anymore. He stood up, lifting me by my arms along the way. I was led over to the sofa and carefully placed down. 'What's going on?' he asked, rolling up my dress to look at my legs.

I still had a few unhealed cuts and bruises from my unplanned night trip. They were nothing compared to the state of Sam's back.

'What happened here, Maggie?' he demanded, in a soft way.

I placed my hands on his shoulders and kissed his cheek.

He raised his eyes. They smiled at me. 'Don't distract me. What happened to you? You look like you've had a fight with the forest. Did you do this helping me?'

'I need to tell you something.'

We both glanced over at the door, as someone was knocking.

Sam got up to open the door.

Standing outside was Claris and her Guardians. She marched straight in.

I stood up quickly. 'Guide Claris,' I greeted quietly.

She didn't beat around the bush. 'Maggie, you are to come with me,' she said flatly. 'It is your turn to be punished.'

Sam flashed me a concerned look.

I said what we were both thinking. 'Punished? What for?'

'Defiance,' she said.

Left and Right stepped forward and stood either side of me.

Claris gave them a slight nod.

They each held one of my elbows.

'When was I defiant?' I asked. I needed to know what they knew.

'Before your husband's punishment,' she replied. 'You spoke back to Rochelle. You didn't think you would get away with that, did you?'

I had no idea. No one had spoken to me since Sam's beating. I felt worried for myself but relieved it wasn't about Beatrix. I silently prayed that Sam would not step in the way.

'Am I going to be whipped?' I asked. I had to know.

'No,' said Claris. 'You're going into confinement for ten hours for your crime.'

Neither Sam nor I knew exactly what that meant.

'Everyone, follow me,' said Claris, leaving. 'Including you, Sam. You need to see what you have done to your wife. After all, this is all your fault.'

I looked down at my clothes. 'I'm in my house dress, Guide Claris,' I reminded her.

She raised her eyebrows at the thin cloth. 'Well, aren't you the lucky one.'

I was led outside into the heat. Claris was up front, and Sam behind me. We were all quiet.

We walked along a pathway and stopped close to a small wooden hut the size of a large dog's kennel.

'You will stay inside there, Maggie,' said Claris. 'Do you understand?'

I could see Sam's eyes widen with worry. I nodded at Claris.

'You will be released in ten hours,' she said. 'You will not be permitted to speak, eat, or drink while inside. You will be guarded at all times. If you break any of the confinement rules, you will stay in there longer.'

I stared down at the small enclosed space. I saw the cupboard under the stairs. I was all right. Its stuffy darkness had become my friend.

Claris nodded at Left and Right, and they led me towards the hut. 'The best way to sit in there is to huddle your knees into your chest,' she said, smiling at me like she was being helpful.

I bent down and shuffled myself inside and sat how she had told me to. I already felt cramped, not to mention hot.

The door closed on me and I heard the chain rattle into place, locking me inside. Then, I heard Claris speak to Sam.

'You did this to Maggie. I hope you learn a valuable lesson. You are to come back here in ten hours and take your wife home. Do you understand?'

Sam said, 'Yes, Guide Claris.'

'Once this is over, you will both be cleared of all charges, then things can get back to normal around here,' said Claris. 'There will be no more mention of any of this.'

Sam said, 'Yes, Guide Claris.'

'Now, go home, and when you come back, make sure you bring some water with you. She will need it, but not too much. A little drop at a time.'

I heard footsteps walking away. I couldn't see much, as there weren't many cracks in the old wood. I figured Left and Right were still outside. My hunched neck was already starting to ache, as were my scrunched legs. The air was hot and stuffy, and I knew I would feel faint very soon.

The darkness inside didn't bother me. I had previous experience of sitting in dark, confined spaces. The struggle was going to be the heat, the cramps, and worrying about what Sam might do.

21

The noise of the clinking chain caused me to stir. A bright light hit my blurred vision. I heard a muffled voice and felt hands grab my shoulders. Someone was trying to make me stand up, but I couldn't. My body hurt, and my head felt light and dizzy. I was shivering, but I felt hot. I wanted to throw up, but everything went dark again.

* * *

Water dripped onto my lips. My eyes flickered open and closed. I couldn't stop shivering. My skin felt wet. I glanced at my shoulder to see a tee-shirt covering me. I was in bed. My bed. Sam's face came in and out of sight. He was saying something to me.

'Take some more water, Maggie.'

A cool cloth rested on my head. It felt nice, soothing. Something powdery touched my tongue followed by some water. I swallowed. I shivered. The covers were pulled up closer to my throat. I watched Sam. He wasn't smiling. His serious face faded.

* * *

I was swallowing warm soup. There were mashed vegetables in its liquid. I could only take a few mouthfuls. I felt sick, and my head hurt. I couldn't stop shivering.

'You'll be okay soon, Maggie.' I heard Sam say.

I wanted my body to stop shaking. I wanted the heat to go away. I wanted my head to feel right. Nothing felt right. The warm cloth on my forehead was replaced with a cool one. It felt so good.

'Go back to sleep now,' whispered Sam.

* * *

I woke up feeling damp. I reached my arm out of the bed covers and removed the warm cloth from my head. I flopped it down beside me. My stomach felt empty and weak. I really fancied a cup of tea. I sat myself up slightly, and it was then that I realised how weak the rest of me felt. My head was light and parts of me hurt. I stretched my neck and looked around the bedroom.

I was alone.

I heard movement coming from the kitchen.

'Sam,' I called. My throat was coarse.

Sam was in the doorway before I had a chance to get out of bed.

'Whoa, Maggie!' he said, rushing over to me. 'Stay there for now. You're weak. You still need to rest.'

He tucked me back in, propped up my pillow, and sat down at the end of the bed, next to my feet.

'How are you feeling?' he asked softly.

'Hungry.'

He smiled. 'That's a good sign. We'll start you with something light and build you up. You threw up last night, so we don't want a repeat of that.'

'I did?' I had no memory of it.

He gave a slight shrug. 'Not to worry.' He then got up to come closer towards me. He reached out his hand to feel my forehead. 'Your temperature feels back to normal. That's good.' He studied my face for a few seconds. 'How about a cup of tea?'

'And toast?'

He nodded. 'Yeah, and toast.'

* * *

By dinnertime, I had showered, with Sam watching me in case I fainted, and had been dressed in another one of his tee-shirts and encouraged to eat a cheese sandwich. I was also allowed to help him clean his back.

My legs were still hurting, but I felt awake and able to walk around the house without feeling faint, and Sam had started to relax around me.

We sat and ate our dinner, which was a small meal consisting of hard-boiled eggs, salad, and bread. Sam kept topping up my glass with water and shooting worried glances at me every so often.

I had so much to tell him, but I wasn't sure when the right time would be.

He looked so worn through, even more than when he came out of the Ward. How could I put this news on him? Did he have the strength to deal with the truth?

Did I?

I only realised I had stopped eating when Sam questioned me about that fact.

'Do you feel sick again, Maggie?'

I shook my head. 'No. I'm okay.'

'You don't look okay. Should I help you back to bed?'

'No. I'm okay.'

'Please, try to eat a bit more then.'

I sipped my water.

Sam put his knife and fork down. 'Tell me what to do, Maggie.'

I looked over at him. 'It's all right, Sam. There isn't anything to do. I'm just tired, that's all.'

He nodded slightly.

'How is your back feeling?' I asked.

'I'm more worried about you right now,' he replied.

'Did you take your antibiotics while I was…' my voice trailed away.

'I did.'

I sipped some more water.

He took a slow and steady breath while looking directly in my eyes. 'Tell me what's inside your head.'

I wanted to, but I couldn't be sure.

'We talk about everything,' he reminded me. 'I'm on your side.'

I stayed silent.

'Maggie, whatever you want to say, you can just say it. We'll get through it, together.'

'What if I told you something bad?'

He shrugged. A look of concern washed across his face. 'You have my word, it will stay between us.'

I looked him straight in the eyes. 'Do I really have your word, Sam?'

He gave a slight smile and blushed. 'Maggie, you have my heart.'

So, I told him. I told him everything. I didn't skip bits. I didn't add bits. I just told him the facts and then I waited. I waited for his face to change. I waited for his judgement of me to change. I waited for his world to fall out from beneath him. I just waited.

There was a short silence, but it felt long. I knew it was a lot to process because I was still processing it all. There wasn't an hour that went by where I didn't think of Beatrix. Every time I closed my eyes, I saw Tom's icy face. I wished so hard for it not to be real. I wanted to leave so badly, and to take Sam away with me. Start a new life together, away from Mindforder, away from this nightmare. I just wanted him. I prayed he wanted me just as much.

Sam was sitting still, just staring at his plate. He finally adjusted his position. He faced me and reached out a hand and held mine across the table.

'Maggie,' he said quietly. 'I'll build us that raft. We're getting out of here.'

22

Mackenzie

I sat on my bedroom floor with a pen in one hand and a notepad in the other. I stared blankly at the empty page. Nothing was coming to mind. I had decided I would write a short poem and put it up in my window for Adam. It would say how sorry I was and how much I missed him.

Sam was right. I didn't take chances, and I was letting life pass me by. I had left the mess I made with Adam for too long. It was time *Old Comfy Slippers* knew exactly how I felt about him.

The blank paper seemed to be mocking me. I glanced up at the window, then over at my door as my dad jogged by.

'Dad,' I called out.

He jogged back and continued to jog on the spot in the doorway.

I frowned at the beads of sweat lining his receding hairline and hoped they stayed put. The thought of his sweat flicking into my room turned my stomach.

'What's up, baby girl?' He stared down at the digital band on his wrist that was apparently timing him. 'I'm in the middle of my routine.'

Dad stated the obvious, as usual.

'Dad, how do you write a poem?'

He scrunched his nose up and looked down at the notepad in my hand. 'Erm… just make some words rhyme.'

'That's it?'

He shrugged, checked his wristband, and added, 'I don't think they all rhyme.'

'Not helpful, Dad.'

‘Well, why would I know? I’m a banker not a poet.’

‘I bet lots of bankers are creative in their spare time.’

He sniffed away his snot. ‘Not me. I’m active.’

I grimaced at his bright blue shorts and matching vest top.

‘What’s this for anyway?’ he asked.

I nodded towards the window. ‘It’s for Adam. I need to tell him I’m sorry.’

‘What, and you can’t just say that?’

‘I’ve tried, but he’s not talking to me, so I thought a poem might get his attention. It’s what he would do if the shoe were on the other foot.’

Dad nodded. ‘Yeah, that’s because he’s good at all that stuff.’

My shoulders slumped. ‘Thanks, Dad.’ I dropped the notepad to the grey carpet beneath me.

‘Life’s a lot easier when you make things simple,’ he said, staring at his wrist again.

‘I wasn’t going to write anything too long.’

He raised his eyebrows as though a thought had just flashed across his mind. It had, but it wasn’t a good one. ‘You could sing out the window to him, if you want to be romantic.’

‘No, Dad. Just no,’ I told him flatly.

There was no way in a million years I was singing out my window to Adam, or anyone. Firstly, I couldn’t sing, and secondly, I wasn’t living in a musical.

‘Anyway,’ I added, ‘I don’t want to be romantic. I just want him to believe me when I say I’m sorry.’

Dad shrugged. ‘Well, I’m sorry to say, but if he won’t listen to you say the words, he’s not going to take any notice just because you write them down.’

‘He might,’ I said quickly. ‘He likes that sort of thing.’

‘Just tell him you love him. That should open his eyes.’

‘Dad!’ I felt quite shocked to hear my dad say that. ‘Who says I love him?’

He scoffed. ‘Oh please! You have spoken to the boy through your bedroom window pretty much every day since we moved here. You two are practically inseparable.’ He paused. ‘What did you do to him?’

I lowered my head in shame and twiddled my pen. ‘I don’t want to talk about it.’

‘Fair enough,’ he mumbled. ‘At least your mother is pleased that she hasn’t had to hoover up any gravel for the last few weeks. That’s not an easy task in the snow, you know.’

My eyes remained fixed on my doorway for a while after my dad had jogged off.

I knew my mum wasn’t really pleased. She liked having an excuse to go outside to show off whatever new Dyson she had.

‘Normal people would use a broom,’ I once told her.

‘Normal people don’t throw grit at other people’s windows,’ had been her flat response.

I glanced back at the empty notepad, thinking poems can’t be that hard. Just a few words saying sorry, make them rhyme. Adam will love it.

‘Dear Adam. No, that’s not right. No one starts a poem with dear, or do they?’

I picked up my phone and did a quick check online. ‘How to write a poem,’ I mumbled to the phone.

I looked at three short poems and then I got bored. I went back to staring at the notepad, wondering what rhymed with Adam. Madam.

‘Why would I write madam?’

The singing wasn’t sounding so bad now. It couldn’t be any worse than this.

I felt agitated.

'Right. That's it. Enough faffing around.' I was determined to write something.

I'm sorry I hurt you
I'll never desert you
You're my best friend
Please don't let this be the end

I read it over and wondered if I should add Happy New Year. I decided against it, as it was January 3rd. I read it over again.

'That should do the trick.'

I rolled under my bed to forage for the roll of sticky tape I knew was there somewhere from when I was wrapping Christmas presents. 'Aha! Got it.'

Christmas had come and gone so fast this year, or rather, last year. I didn't see anything of Adam. Sam had his mum stay a few days at Moreton Hall, and I was given two weeks off. Two weeks spent indoors with just my parents. I had given up my job at the pub, even though I had felt guilty about leaving poor old Harvey in the festive lurch. At least that's what I thought at first, but as it turned out, he had replaced me within the blink of an eye. He wasn't poor old Harvey after all. He didn't even try to persuade me to stay, and I had spent so much time overthinking that conversation.

I banged my head on the bed as I got up. I took it as a reminder to stop thinking about the past, and be present.

I used my teeth to rip off some tape, tore out my poetic page, and stuck it to the window. The wording was nice and big. There was no way Adam would miss my gesture.

I glanced at my phone as it started to vibrate. George was calling me.

'Mac, I know you don't start back for a couple more days, but come in now. We've had a visitor.'

* * *

George's cagey message had irritated me all the way to Moreton Hall. He flat out refused to tell me what was going on over the phone, so I had little choice but to get dressed and go to work. The curiosity was destroying my soul.

Victoria gave nothing away with her face as she said hello to me on her way across the hallway.

I hung up my coat and hat and went off to find George. He was in the room where I had my unconventional interview. I secretly called that room the hunting lodge.

'George, what's going on?' I asked, entering and closing the door behind me. 'Who is here?'

George was sitting on the sofa, reading through some files. He waved me towards him. I sat down by his side.

'He's gone now,' he said quietly.

'Who?'

'The couple who own this place have always been in contact with police who investigate cult crimes, that sort of thing. They lost their twin sons to a cult years ago. That's why they started this place.'

I nodded, awaiting more.

George continued, 'Someone from the team came here this morning to talk to Sam.'

'Is Sam ready for that?'

George shrugged. 'Victoria seems to think so.'

'What do you think?'

'I think Sam's come a long way over the last few months. I'm not sure he's ready to talk to the police. Victoria's been holding it off since he arrived, but this special team always want to talk to the guests at some point.'

'Did Sam talk to them?'

'Yeah, but it didn't last long. I don't know what he said. I wasn't in the room. It was just Sam and the officer. I do know that they have always had a keen interest in Mindforder. They would love Sam's help in bringing that organisation down.'

'I don't know if Sam would help with that. He still says good things about them.'

George nodded down at the files on his lap. 'I'm just going through everything Sam has ever said. Plus, I got the officer's notes. They have to inform us on how Sam acted, what he said, and so on.'

I glanced at the files. 'How far have you got?'

'Not far. I'm just making my own notes. Victoria thought it would be a good idea if you went and spoke to Sam.'

'Me?'

'Yes, Mac. Everyone here knows he responds better to you.'

'He does?' I wasn't trained in trauma like everyone at Moreton Hall. I was just me. The dinner lady and tea girl.

* * *

Sam was sitting on a chair in his room, staring out the window at the cold lake. He was dressed in a navy tracksuit and had a white blanket draped over his shoulders.

I didn't feel cold. I thought the room was quite warm, but he obviously felt a chill.

'Mac,' he questioned, without turning to see who was standing in his doorway.

'Yes, it's me.'

He remained staring out the window. ‘You’re not due back for another couple of days.’ His voice was low and quite faded.

I entered the room and sat on the bed. ‘I know, but I heard you had a visitor.’

‘He didn’t stay long.’

‘You didn’t want to talk to him?’

His head shook slightly as he lowered it to look at his lap. ‘Not really.’

‘Do you want to talk about it to me?’

His fingers twiddled with the edging of his blanket. ‘I’ve told you everything. There’s nothing left to say.’

I tried to keep my voice upbeat. ‘I think the police just want to help you bring down Mindforder.’

He turned sharply to look at me. ‘I don’t want any part of that.’

I was a little surprised. ‘But what about Buddy?’

He shrugged. ‘Nothing I can do about him.’

‘The police might be able to do something, with your help.’

He looked back at his lap again.

It was obvious that he didn’t want to talk about any of it. Reliving his time with Mindforder wasn’t easy. It only made him think about Maggie. She was gone, and he struggled with that. I knew he cared little for himself, let alone the people of Mindforder or the police. It was too soon. Victoria was wrong. Sam wasn’t ready to move in that direction. He was still processing everything that had happened to him. Even I knew that.

‘Do you want me to leave you alone, Sam?’ I asked softly.

‘No. I’d rather you stayed.’

‘Okay.’

He glanced over at me. 'Am I keeping you from anything?'

I laughed to myself. 'Only bad poetry.'

He frowned, and I shook my hand to wave away the comment.

'It's my fault she's dead, you know,' he said quietly.

I raised my head to look directly at him. His sudden statement had taken me aback. Obviously, he did have things he wanted to say.

'How is it your fault?' I asked gently.

'I built that raft.'

He had already told me how the raft was Beatrix's idea. 'You were asked to do that.'

'It was a stupid idea.'

'You didn't have a lot of choice, Sam.' I didn't feel I should be reminding him.

He went silent. Perhaps in thought.

'How else were you to get off that island?' I asked. 'You tried. That's all.'

'That's not all, Mackenzie, and you know that. Maggie died because of that raft. Because of me.'

I watched him take a deep breath and steady his shaky hands. I really wished that he would believe it wasn't his fault. They had both agreed to escape. They both agreed to build that raft. They both got on it without force. They both knew they had no idea where they were or where they would end up. They were desperate and in danger.

His hand shot up to cover his mouth as a breathy cry escaped his lips. 'Oh, I'm sorry.'

I hurried around to him and dropped to my knees in between his legs.

'It's okay, Sam.'

Tears fell from his eyes to mingle in with his fingers that were clutching his mouth. 'I'm sorry, Mackenzie,' he sobbed.

'Please, stop saying sorry,' I said softly. 'You have nothing to be sorry for.'

He was trying hard to roll back his tears, to control his breathing, and to numb his pain, but it was all there, needing to be recognised.

'I just miss her so much,' he breathed out. 'I shouldn't be here.'

I didn't know which here he meant.

'I don't deserve to live,' he added. 'It's not fair.'

I looked at his tear-stained face as he slowly calmed himself. His sore eyes rolled towards mine.

'When they told me she had died…' He hesitated. 'I've got nothing left, Mackenzie. Nothing left inside of me.'

I didn't blurt out the first thing that came to mind because nothing came to mind. I had no idea what to say. George would have wise words, or textbook words, but I couldn't even reach deep within me to write a decent enough poem to Adam. How was I supposed to handle Sam's shredded heart?

'I'm sorry, Sam,' I managed, handing him a tissue from my cardigan pocket. 'I wish I could take away your pain.' I meant that. Those words came from my heart. I could feel my emotion, or maybe it was his emotion. Either way, emotion filled me.

He wiped his face, then his gentle eyes met mine. He gave me a slight smile.

I smiled back.

He leant forward and kissed me on the mouth.

I wasn't expecting that, and I had no idea what to do about it. He was so lovely, and I cared so deeply for him, but his warm and gentle kiss felt strange. Slightly off, as though it were George kissing me. I found myself not moving away. I waited until he pulled back.

Sam looked at me with a blank expression. 'That wasn't right, was it?'

I pulled in my lips and slowly shook my head.

'I'm sorry, Mackenzie.' He was genuine. I could tell.

I reached forward and held his hands in mine. 'It's all right, Sam. Sometimes we just want to feel love, that's all.'

He looked deep within my eyes. I felt like he was searching for something. He then looked over at the window.

I got off my knees and sat on the edge of the bed.

'I'm not confused,' he told me.

'I know. You just miss Maggie.'

His eyes narrowed as he turned to me. 'You don't understand, Mackenzie.'

I shrugged. 'Maybe not.'

'I shouldn't have kissed you,' he said, sitting up straight and furrowing his brow. 'Have I ruined things between us now?'

'No,' I said simply. 'We're fine. Everything is fine. Well, you know, as fine as it can be.' I muffled a laugh.

His eyes were examining me again. Whenever he stared at me like that, it always made me feel both warm and uncomfortable. I wanted to know what he was thinking when he had that look, but I never wanted to ask.

'I wonder what Maggie would say about that?' he questioned himself.

I couldn't answer. I didn't know her. I knew Adam wouldn't be too pleased.

'When was the last time you saw her?'

He stared forward. He was back there. With her. 'On the raft.'

23

Maggie

I had imagined the first night on the raft to be the scariest time for us, but it wasn't. It was the most romantic night of my life.

High above, in the night-time sky, the full moon shone down. No clouds masked its view, and a million twinkling stars filled almost every other available space.

Down below, the dark ocean was calmly swaying the rickety raft.

I thought it would be eerie. That the open sea would make me vulnerable and alert, but I was lying on my back, upon a sheet, watching the sky, and feeling tranquil, like I was in a safe and friendly dream.

Sam was relaxed at my side, smiling.

The darkness surrounding us did little to intimidate. We were free. Nothing else mattered. Nothing else touched us. What awaited us back on the Island was far worse than anything Mother Nature could do to us. We trusted *she* was on our side. We didn't have anyone or anything else helping us.

A warm breeze wafted over our bodies, soothing our souls. We were both peaceful.

I smiled at the moon, and then I turned my head to look at Sam.

He held the same dreamy gaze as me. 'The sky looks incredible.' His voice was as relaxed as his body.

'It feels magical, Sam.'

He turned and smiled warmly at me. 'Would it sound cheesy if I said every moment spent with you is magical?'

I giggled. ‘About as cheesy as the moon.’

He glanced up at the sky and breathed out a laugh. ‘Oh, Maggie, what are we doing?’

I gave a slight shrug. ‘Moving house.’

He laughed. ‘Well, that’s one way of putting it.’

I had a horrible thought. ‘I hope we don’t go around in a circle and end up washed up back on the Island.’

He scrunched his face. ‘Let’s pray we don’t.’

We held hands, closed our eyes, and said a silent prayer that asked for guidance, safety, and freedom.

Sam raised my hand and kissed the back of it, then placed it back down again. ‘Everything’s going to be okay now, Maggie.’

I smiled at his optimism. I knew I had to keep the faith.

He carefully turned on his side, leant up on his elbow, and rested the side of his face on his hand. He was looking down at me.

I gazed into his warm eyes. ‘What you thinking, Sam?’

‘How beautiful you are.’

I blushed.

He laughed slightly. ‘You’re not very good with compliments.’ He shook his head a bit. ‘You’re going to have to get used to them.’

I rolled my eyes. ‘Am I?’

He smiled, then stared out into the darkness.

I reached my hand up to stroke his arm, drawing his attention back to me.

He studied my face for a moment. I closed my eyes, and he leaned down and kissed my eyelids.

I opened my eyes and smiled.

The intensity lingered between us.

He then slipped effortlessly from relaxed to serious. ‘I’m sorry for any time I might have made you feel unwanted back on the Island.' He took a steady breath that sounded like a sigh. 'I just wanted to get things right. I wanted to be the man you deserve to have. I still want to be that man.'

I had never thought too much about love before I met him. Sex had always been flat and meaningless. My heart had never fluttered. My body had never been lifted by a light-headed feeling. I entered an uncharted territory when I met Sam. The newness of kindness and warmth disorientated me at times. The passion between us had completely carried me away to fairy tale land, where the sun had a smiley face and birds flew in circles while singing sweetly around my giddy head.

I turned and placed my hand on his chest. I could feel him breathing.

He looked down at my fingertips stroking him. He was avoiding meeting my eyes.

The warm air wafted over us. I licked my lips, tasting the salt. I watched the corners of his mouth curl upwards until they stopped at a bashful smile.

'You're everything to me, Sam,' I said quietly.

He swallowed hard. His mouth was dry. His eyes gave me an enquiring look.

I tried not to make any facial expressions. I needed him to feel like he could say anything to me. I wanted to absorb his new independence. Be a silent partner in his liberation.

He took a moment. A moment that belonged only to him. I could tell that he didn't want to express himself incorrectly. His cracked voice entered the night. 'I want to be your equal, Maggie.'

My body softened. I tugged his arm, pulling him closer to me.

His body leaned over mine, carefully. We were aware of the delicate contraption we were floating on. His eyes gazed down into mine.

I could see that his face was already starting to look hot and damp.

'If I say you are, will you ever believe me?' I asked.

There was a chance that he would remain stuck within the laws of Mindforder. It was already haunting me.

He gave a slight nod down towards my opened mouth. 'I will.'

I felt his warm breath hit my cheeks. He smelled like the apple he had eaten just before we set sail.

The bottom half of his body adjusted itself to mine. He was holding off from pressing against me.

'You're my equal, Sam.'

My words hit his heart. It was as obvious as the big bright moon above us.

I didn't want him to speak anymore. I knew I would barely register any words that left his mouth. My whole being had wandered far from conversation. I slowly leaned up, forcing his movement backwards.

He quietly watched me remove my indoor dress. He lifted his tee-shirt over his head and removed his bottoms.

I lowered my back to meet with the white sheet again. We slowly removed our underwear.

He scanned my pale skin. All of the parts that were once dangerous to touch no longer had restrictions. There was nothing to be afraid of. There was no defiance. No hidden excitement. No thought of regret.

I wound my legs around him, holding him close to me.

His lips parted. He mouthed the words, 'I love you.'

My body weakened beneath him. My heart wept from the impact of his tenderness. It overwhelmed me.

‘I love you,’ I whispered.

Our bodies moved as the subtle waves gently rocked the raft. I watched his chest slowly inhale, then exhale.

His fingertips lightly brushed my hair behind my ear, and then he lowered his face until his mouth was pressed softly against mine.

At first, he was tentative. Taking his time to explore every touch, every second with me. Then, his passion appeared, and I surrendered every part of myself to him. I would have done anything for him. Anything he asked, but he didn’t ask for anything from me. He just gave to me, making sure that no part of me felt unwanted, unloved.

24

I woke up in a hospital bed and the first person I saw was my sister. Her face looked solemn and disappointed. It also looked a lighter shade of brown than it used to look. I wasn't sure if she had been trying to bleach her skin again, or if it was her makeup, or just my blurry eyes.

We had different dads, who had different skin tones. She had never been happy about her colour, or any other part of her. I never understood why. She was tall, slim, and so pretty. Definitely model material. I, on the other hand, had a plain and boring face and often looked like I belonged to vampires.

It took me a minute to gather my bearings. I definitely wasn't in the Ward, but I was in a ward.

My sister was saying something to me, but her words weren't connecting to my brain. She sounded muffled.

A tall man pulled her to one side. I heard his deep voice. He called her by her proper name, Shannon. We always called her Shane. He told her not to go on at me, and now was not the time, and to let me rest.

I didn't know who he was, but I liked him straight away.

A nurse leant over my face and shone a light in my eyes. She smelled nice, of something mildly sweet. She mumbled something and walked away.

I looked back at the glare of my sister. She was unimpressed about something.

My head felt a bit woozy, so I wasn't sure if that's why my sister looked older. It was definitely her though. She didn't look or smell as sweet as the nurse.

The man standing with her looked pleasant enough. Older than me, with soft blonde hair and kind eyes. I warmed to his kind eyes. Lovely, kind, gentle eyes looking at me with concern.

I shot up. 'Sam,' I cried. Everything around me started to spin.

* * *

They thought I couldn't hear them having a conversation about me in the living room, but I could hear their muffled voices, and I wanted to know what was going on.

Nobody had told me anything about Sam since I woke up in hospital. I had been living at my sister's house for two days, and enough was enough.

I barged into their space and demanded they talk to me, not about me. I wasn't a child. I deserved to know what was going on.

One minute I was half-dead, floating on a raft in the middle of the ocean with Sam, the next thing I knew, I was in hospital, and Sam was nowhere to be seen, and my sister had appeared with a strange man in tow, and now I was in their cosy two-bed terrace house somewhere in London.

'He's dead, Mags,' said my sister coldly. 'That man you were with, Sam, he's dead.'

Her flooring was dark oak laminated panels. They smelled like dust and felt cool against my face. I watched the tears drip down, creating a tiny puddle on the wood. My knotted stomach split as sweat crept into my hair. A woman was screaming, a loud, high-pitched screech of a sound. She sounded distant and tortured. Was that noise coming from me? Hands were on my body, tugging my arms, my shoulders. I was floating above the fake floor. I watched it slowly leave me behind. Suddenly, I was alone in a bed. The space around me felt like it went on forever, and I was drowning inside of it. I could barely breathe. I closed my eyes, in hope that the action would take away the strange feeling whirling inside me.

* * *

I opened my letter and smiled at the documents staring back at me. Everything was in place.

'This is a stupid idea,' said my sister.

'I don't care what you think, Shane,' I told her flatly. 'I'm going to Ireland, and I'm going to find Sam's grave.'

She huffed. 'It's been ages. Why bother now?' She turned to her husband. 'Tell her, Teddy.'

Teddy jumped in. 'Shannon, don't say it like that. Maggie needed time to heal. Plus, you know she has to stay hidden from that lot.'

Shane pointed down at my cornflakes sitting on the table. 'See, what about that, Mags? What if those people are looking for you? They might be there in Ireland, waiting. This ain't a good idea.'

'Shane, I don't care,' I snapped.

All I cared about was putting some flowers down wherever Sam had been laid to rest. I wanted to say my own goodbye. If anyone from Mindforder found me and killed me, so be it. I really didn't care for my life. I just wanted to be with Sam.

I stared at the soggy cereal in front of me as my brother-in-law led my annoying sister away from me. I could hear Sam's voice in my head.

'Eat something, Maggie.'

I smiled.

‘Soon,’ I whispered into the bowl.

I had my flight booked, my hotel paid for, I sort of knew where I was going, and I couldn’t wait to get there. To be closer to him. To sit with him for a while. To tell him that I was sorry. It was all my stupid fault. What did we know about rafts and oceans? What were we thinking?

Teddy’s hand touched my shoulder. ‘I’ll take you to the airport, Maggie. Don’t worry. It’ll be okay. Shannon’s just worried about those Mind people. She does care about you, you know.’

‘Thanks, Ted,’ I said, smiling up at him.

* * *

The drive to the airport didn’t really take that long, but it felt like forever. Little did Shane and Teddy know, but I planned to stay in Ireland. I would get a job in Dublin and live there until the day I died.

I hoped that day wasn’t too far away. I found no joy in living. My life was empty.

Ireland was Sam’s home, so it would be mine. It was all I could think about. I would find out where his family had placed him, and I would take tea and toast and sit with him. He would laugh about the cold toast. I could hear his laughter. I could see his smile.

Shane had stayed behind. She seemed vacant and at a loss for words as I walked out the door. Although, she did give me a big hug, which was unusual for her.

Teddy was quiet on the drive, but I didn’t mind. My mind was occupied by Sam.

I thanked my kind brother-in-law for paying for my trip. He had been generous allowing me to live in his home rent-free, eat his food, and slouch around all day doing very little to help out.

Teddy's eyes filled with remorse as I got out of his silver car and said goodbye to him through the window.

'Maggie, wait,' he said, grabbing my arm. 'There's something you need to know before you go.'

I rolled my eyes. 'If this is about Shane…'

He cut me off, 'No. It's about Sam.'

He had my attention. 'Have you found out where he is?'

He shook his head. 'No, Maggie. I don't know where he is, but I do that he's not really dead.'

I think my heart just stopped. I couldn't feel it anymore. I couldn't feel anything anymore. Teddy just said something that sounded like *not really dead*, but he couldn't have said that. That made no sense.

He took a deep breath. 'We were told to tell you that for your own safety.'

What was he going on about?

'Maggie,' he said quietly, 'Sam's alive.'

* * *

As soon as I had unpacked my small number of belongings in my hotel room in Dublin, I left for the town where Sam grew up.

The train ride seemed to take forever. I willed it to hurry. I felt rushed and pulled back at the same time. A thousand thoughts filled my head, giving me a headache. I didn't know what to believe anymore. I just had to find Sam's house and see if he was there. If anyone was there. If anyone had the answers to my many questions.

The train arrived at Donstown. I asked in the first shop I saw outside the station how I would get to Castlebrook. I was directed to a bus top, where I waited at least an hour for the small bus to arrive. I told the driver I didn't know where exactly I was going. He smiled and asked me who I was going to see in Castlebrook. Apparently, it wasn't a big place, and the driver, who told me to call him Big Chris, seemed to know everyone and everywhere.

I was wary about mentioning Sam's name, so I said, 'Mary Whittington.' I hoped she used the same last name as her son.

Big Chris grinned widely, revealing his crooked teeth and dimples. 'I know where you need.'

As we were the only two people on the bus, I sat up front, close to him, and listened to him happily chat away about the area. I stared out the window at the large open fields we passed by. Sam's childhood home was worlds apart from the concrete jungle I grew up in.

Big Chris had loads of gossip, but I wasn't taking it all in. He seemed harmless enough, but I knew there were millions of members of Mindforder, so I played it safe when he asked me about myself. I told him my name was Jane, and that I was a distant relative of Mary's, who had finally come to visit. He seemed fulfilled by that information.

The bus came to a stop along a narrow road.

'Follow that road up there,' said Big Chris, pointing me in the right direction. 'The house is just on the other side of that hill. You can't miss it.'

'Thank you, Big Chris,' I said, trying not to smile at saying his name.

'There'll be another bus going back in just over an hour, so you know, Jane.'

'Okay, thanks.' I waved him goodbye.

It was so quiet once the bus vanished out of sight. It was just me, two stone walls, and a narrow road leading uphill.

I smiled at the mass of long green grass growing in the fields around me.

I started to walk while thinking about how Sam might have got to school. Did he take the bus? Did he cycle, maybe? I bet his mum drove him. Although, I wasn't sure how a car would even fit along the road I was on, it was so narrow.

The whole area filled me with a warm and fuzzy feeling. I was walking in Sam's footsteps. His invisible footprints were all along the road. I peered over my shoulder as, just for a second, I sensed him there, walking behind me.

I felt a rush of joy fill me. I upped my pace. It turned into a jog and then a run. I was breathless by the time I reached the top of the hill.

'Whoa!'

Down the other side, in the near distance, was a big white house. It looked very expensive. Not the type of home you would see in my neighbourhood. It looked old but well maintained. I laughed to myself.

I visualised Sam walking out the front door and seeing me standing here. I couldn't wait to see if that would happen. I had to know if he was inside. If he really was alive.

'Please be alive, Sam,' I whispered into the fresh, cool air.

I ran all the way and took a moment to catch my breath before knocking on the large white door.

There was no answer. I saw a bell and pressed that. I understood that it was a large home, and it might take someone a little while to reach the door. I didn't want my impatience to come across as rude.

I jumped slightly as the door opened.

A little old lady with white hair and rosy cheeks smiled up at me. She had a friendly, warm face.

‘Hello, dear,’ she said. Her accent was just as soft as Sam’s.

‘Hello, I’m…’ I froze.

She widened her beady eyes. ‘You are?’

My mind had caved in on me. I was suddenly lost for words. What kind of conversation was I about to have? I thought about Big Chris, how he wouldn’t have had this problem. He would have known what to say. Why couldn’t I speak?

‘Are you feeling all right, child?’ she asked gently.

I pointed behind me. ‘I ran all the way,’ I said breathlessly.

She peered around me. ‘Did you get lost?’

‘I don’t think so,’ I managed to say. Words were coming back. ‘I’m looking for Sam.’

The kindness in her eyes snapped shut. ‘There’s no one here by that name.’

She went to close the door on me. I panicked. I put my foot in the way and watched her eyes roll nervously down at my brown boot.

‘Do I need to call the police.’ She wasn’t asking.

‘I’m sorry. I just want to see Sam. Please. Just tell him Maggie is here.’

She paused, then repeated her first statement.

‘Where is he?’ I practically begged. I knew she could see the tears in my eyes.

‘I think you’re lost, dear,’ she said sympathetically.

I took a deep breath. ‘They told me he died,’ I blurted out. ‘All this time, I thought he was dead. Just tell me he’s not dead. Please, just tell me that much.’

She seemed to be studying me. ‘I’m so sorry, but there’s no Sam here. You have to go now.’

I knew she was wary. If my life was in danger, so was Sam's.

'I'm not from Mindforder,' I told her. 'I'm Maggie. I'm his wife. Okay, so maybe I am from Mindforder, but I'm not with them anymore. Me and Sam, Sam and I, we tried to escape, you see. We made a raft. I woke up in hospital. They said Sam died. I came here to put flowers on his grave, but then I found out he wasn't really dead. It had all been a lie to protect me. My family lied. Everyone lied.' I started to cry.

I turned away from her glare and flopped down to the porch step. My head was in my hands, and my tears would not stop falling down onto my knees. I was lost. Lost on Sam's doorstep. I didn't know what to do next. Where to go. Who to turn to.

'Oh, Sam, where are you?' I mumbled.

I felt a hand rest gently on my back. 'Maggie, you say?'

I slowly raised my weary head to see that those kind eyes had returned.

The old lady waved me towards her. 'You had better come inside.'

25

Mackenzie

It was Valentine's Day, or rather, night, and I still hadn't heard anything from Adam. My poem was still firmly stuck to my bedroom window, not that it mattered. I had no idea if he had seen it or not. I wasn't sure if he bothered opening his blind anymore.

I was hiding behind the window frame in my dad's office, watching Adam doing his lengths in the pool. I was right in the middle of wondering if he thought about me anymore, when my mum walked in.

'You know that makes you a stalker, don't you?'

She made me jump. I spun around to face her.

'I'm not a stalker.'

She nodded sympathetically at me.

I frowned.

Mum stepped forward and hugged me. Her warm, chubby arms soothed my aching heart. I inhaled the mild lavender smell coming from her face moisturiser and smiled deeply to myself.

'Mum,' I mumbled into her shoulder. 'I really miss him.'

She pulled back and held a soft stare. 'Then, stop staring at him and go and do something about it.'

'Easy for you to say.'

She raised her eyebrows at me.

I huffed. 'I've tried, Mum. He's blocked me from his life.'

'So, unblock yourself.'

'How?'

She gave a slight nod towards the window. 'If it were me, I'd go over there right now while he's stuck in the middle of that pool with nowhere to go, and I'd spill my guts, and he'd have no choice but to listen.'

I grinned. 'Spill your guts?'

She shrugged. 'Why not? Get it all out there, I say. Let him know exactly how you feel, what he's missing out on, and tell him it's the last time you're going to try talking to him. That way, when you walk away, it'll be up to him to figure out whether or not he'll miss you.'

'I think we can both safely say, he doesn't miss me.'

'You haven't given him a chance to miss you yet. You're always texting him, or ringing him, and don't think I haven't noticed that you have that poem still stuck in your window. Take it down, Mackenzie.'

She had a point. I was always trying. Adam was always ignoring. There was no balance. He hadn't had a chance to know what his life would be like without me because I hadn't left him alone.

'I know where you're coming from, Mum, but we don't play games. We've always been quite straight with each other. I don't want to do stuff to force him into a position where he has to figure out if he misses me or not.'

'Then, go over there right now and be straight. If that's what you two do. Go do exactly that. No games, no fuss, no more dodgy poems.'

I squirmed inside. 'You read my poem?'

'Never mind that,' she said quickly, waving off the invasion of privacy. 'Go get your man, baby girl.'

I glanced down at my pink slippers. 'He won't let me in.'

Mum took my arm and led me over to the side of the window frame. She angled my head to peer down the back of our garden.

'See that bit of hedge about three-quarters of the way down?'

‘Hmm,’ I groaned. My neck was starting to ache.

‘It dips down. Climb over that and then over the fence. Mind yourself, it wobbles a bit. There’s a bench on the other side. You’ll easily get access to their garden that way.’

I turned and grinned. ‘Mum, have you been sneaking into their garden?’

She laughed. ‘No.’

I wasn’t convinced. ‘Then, how do you know about that?’

She looked serious. ‘You have to know all your escape routes, Mackenzie. What if there was some sort of emergency?’

‘What emergency warrants us climbing over the neighbour’s fence?’

‘Fire,’ she said simply. ‘That’s one.’

‘Fire?’ I shook my head.

She stepped away from the window. ‘Look, do you want my help or not?’

My shoulders dropped as I felt my confidence fall flat.

Mum grabbed my shoulders and gave me a slight shake. ‘Come on, Mackenzie. You can do this.’ She leant closer to my face and whispered, ‘You’ve got a big gob. Time to use it.’

And that was pretty much my pep talk.

* * *

Climbing over hedges in the dark wasn’t my idea, but there I was doing it anyway. I was terrified there might be spiders lurking in amongst the greenery, and the sharp wooden fence nestling against it wasn’t there to greet me. Bloody thing, ripped my new green pyjama bottoms. At least my less than graceful tumble down onto the ornate cast-iron bench didn’t hurt too much. I knew I would have a few bruises to show tomorrow for my effort.

I thought about George. He wouldn't believe I did it. I was struggling to believe I was doing it. What was I thinking? This was all Mum's fault, with her big trespassing ideas. I was so glad they didn't have a dog.

I kept low as I hobbled at a great speed across Malorie's fake lawn. I was glad of the artificial grass because I was quite sure that if it was real, I would've, no doubt, set off the sprinklers and got soaked.

I didn't think about the security spotlights.

'Argh!'

Diving into a bush added a new tear to my pyjamas, another bruise to my body, and pulled my hair halfway out of my ponytail. Wasn't the most elegant of things I had done in my life either.

I peeped over to the pool. Adam was still swimming.

'Oh God! I really do look like a stalker. Right! That's it. I've had enough of this,' I whispered into the cold air.

Not a lot else went through my mind up until the moment I found myself face to face with one end of Adam's swimming pool.

'Adds,' I called down to him.

He had almost reached the other end of the pool. He slowed, then stopped, then turned to see me standing there.

I wasn't too sure whether he was surprised, annoyed, or just wondering why I looked like someone who had just been in a tussle with a tree.

Before he got the chance to react, I completely lost my mind.

I didn't realise just how deep the swimming pool was.

I wasn't a confident swimmer, I was much better at drowning, but I was all right, just as long as I could touch the bottom.

I couldn't feel the bottom.

I started to panic.

Running forward, jumping up, flying through the air, and waterbombing a pool is all well and good when you have full-on water confidence, not full-on brain fail.

I coughed and spluttered as the water hit my mouth. My chest was tightening, and my hair was wrapped around my eyes, blinding me.

Every part of me was questioning why I had thought that the only way to grab Adam's attention was to throw myself into his pool. It would have been nice if me and my brain had at least had a quiet chat about it first, but no. Now I was paying the price.

I would have cried from embarrassment, but I was too busy attempting to tread water.

Adam was suddenly there, pulling my frazzled body over to the side of the pool.

His hand removed my flopped hair from my face. 'Are you okay, Mac?'

I sniffed, coughed, and reluctantly rolled my eyes his way.

He was trying not to laugh. He had a stupid grin spread right across his face. That stupid smile was making everything feel better immediately.

'I was trying to get your attention,' I said sheepishly.

I didn't need anyone to tell me how ridiculous I looked. It was a poor attempt at getting noticed, and I was wholeheartedly regretting the situation, except for the fact that I was still being held by one of his arms.

Adam breathed out a laugh. 'Oh, you got my attention.'

Oh Lord, take me now, were the only words that entered my mind.

I wasn't sure if I had started crying or it was the water on my face. 'I just wanted you to notice me.' For some reason, I had acquired some sort of weird high-pitched dolphin tone.

His body moved closer to mine. 'When have I not noticed you?' His voice was soft and gentle.

I sniffed and hoped that my next sentence would sound human. 'You won't talk to me.'

'I'm talking to you now.'

I scoffed. 'Only because you had to save me from drowning.' I sounded pathetic. I knew it. He knew it. The swimming pool knew it.

He grinned. 'And I didn't even get to give you mouth-to-mouth.'

Over a hundred butterflies filled my stomach, or maybe it was all that chlorinated water I swallowed, either way, I felt slightly giddy.

His eyes lowered towards my mouth and stayed there for a few seconds. He then looked back up to my sore eyes. He frowned at my head and reached up to remove a leaf embedded in my hair.

He leant over to put the piece of shrub on the side, and his face came closer to mine. I could feel his breath on my skin. His cheek was practically touching me.

I couldn't resist.

I kissed the side of his face, and then I quickly pulled my head away to look down at the water.

There was no movement between us for a minute or two. I knew I should have just got out of the pool, but I didn't want to. He was holding me, and our bodies were so close. I didn't want to be anywhere else in the world, but the silence was unnerving. I was scared of him rejecting me.

‘I love you, Adam,’ I whispered to the water.

Adam’s face lowered to meet mine. He nuzzled his nose into the side of my cheek and slowly moved his mouth over towards my lips.

I could taste the pool on his skin and feel the warmth in his mouth. His kiss was strong and passionate, filling me with love. I didn’t want it to ever end. I wanted to stay wrapped around him forever.

26

The sound of rain beating against the window pane of Adam's bedroom woke me. It was morning but dark outside. I could see the daybreak trying to burst through the cracks in the partially opened slatted blind. A dreary day outside, but the sun was shining in my heart. I turned to see Adam sleeping. Warmth filled every part of me.

He adjusted his position when he felt me snuggle up under his arm.'Morning, Mac,' he mumbled.

I kissed his chest. 'Morning, Adds.'

He kissed the top of my head.

I rolled up my face so I could see him.

He smiled sleepily at me.

I stroked his face. 'Have I ever told you how much I love you?'

He grinned. 'About a thousand times last night.'

'I love you,' I said happily. 'That makes a thousand and one.'

'I love you too,' he said, rolling over to kiss me.

* * *

Malorie walked into the kitchen to find us eating breakfast, in between loving glances and slight fingertip touching.

We were sitting practically on top of each other at the large glass dining table. We couldn't get any closer than me sitting on his lap, which did cross my mind more than once. I was happy to take our cereal straight back to bed, but Adam said his mum had plans for him that morning.

‘Morning, Mackenzie,’ said Malorie. Her eyes held a slight sparkle. ‘Did you have a good sleep?’

‘Mum!’ said Adam, sighing.

Malorie shrugged. ‘Just asking.’ She poured herself a cup of coffee.

She didn’t make me feel as embarrassed as my own parents would have, had we been in their kitchen, but I still felt a tad awkward.

Adam reached down and held my hand that had flaked to my lap.

Malorie turned to face us. ‘I take it this means you two are together at last?’

I tried not to laugh. ‘At last?’ I questioned.

She nodded into her coffee. ‘It’s been a long time coming.’

Adam blushed. ‘Mum, stop, now.’

I squeezed his hand, and he smiled sheepishly at me.

Malorie approached the table. ‘I’m glad you both sorted it out before I had to make other arrangements.’

Adam stopped looking at me long enough to frown over at his mother. ‘What arrangements?’

She grinned widely. She had a pretty smile that only came out every so often. I liked the way her hard face changed so dramatically whenever she chose to show her feelings.

‘I took the liberty of adding Mackenzie into the details of your trip.’

I was just as confused as Adam.

‘Mum, what have you done?’

Malorie shrugged. ‘I just added her on the flight. I knew I didn’t have to worry about accommodation, seeing how you’ll mostly be staying in my friends’ homes across Europe.’

‘You are?’ I asked him.

He gave a slight nod. 'Mum doesn't want me staying in the hotels provided.' He glanced sideways at her. 'She seems to have friends everywhere. I'll be staying in their empty holiday homes all by myself instead.'

'And they all have swimming pools,' said Malorie. 'And… you won't be by yourself.'

'You want me to go?' I asked her. I felt Adam's hand loosen in mine. I grab a hold of his fingers before they slipped away.

'I thought you might like to,' said Malorie, looking only at her son.

He laughed to himself. 'I cannot believe you planned that.'

'I like to be one step ahead,' said Malorie. She turned to me. 'There's plenty of room for you, Mackenzie. The flights have been paid for. My friend, Jack, has his own plane and will be flying Adam back and forth.'

'I was happy to go with the others. The AOP pay for and arrange everything.'

Malorie waved away the offer. 'No need. We can make our own arrangements.'

I felt overwhelmed. I had no idea plans were being made for me behind my back, nor had I ever been on a private plane before, or any plane, for that matter.

My mum was agoraphobic, so we never went anywhere. She used to tell Dad to take me on holiday, but he didn't think it was fair to go without her, so he never did. He went to London a lot for work and would tell her that he was happy enough with that. Mum was happy in our own quiet town, and she went to a couple of others close by as well. That was as far as her comfort zone stretched.

Adam was quiet while Malorie continued to sell me a free trip around Europe. I got the feeling he wasn't as keen on the idea as she was.

'You want Mac there to babysit me,' he said.

Malorie shook her head. 'Not true. I thought you would want to travel together, that's all. It's a great opportunity for you both to spend some quality time together.'

Adam scoffed. 'Quality time. Really, Mum!'

Somehow, I didn't feel as though the conversation included me. I wanted to go home. I had just spent the most perfect night with Adam, there was no way I was going to sit around and watch my perfect morning with him vanish into thin air.

'What do you think, Mackenzie?' asked Malorie.

I was being forced into the conversation. I wondered what Adam would want me to think. I knew he would want the truth. It's what we did. We had always been pretty straight with each other. Now was no different.

I heard Sam telling me to take a chance, life's too short.

'I'd love to go,' I replied, squeezing his hand.

Adam blushed.

Malorie smiled. 'I'll leave you both to discuss it further.' She brushed her hand over Adam's hair on her passing. 'I'll be in my office.'

He was staring down at his bowl of cereal. 'You don't have to go, Mac, just because she's arranged everything like that. She had no right interfering.'

'I'd love to go with you, Adds, but only if you want me there. I don't want to intrude. This is your tour, your moment to travel, showcasing your talent. I'm happy to stand by your side, but I wouldn't feel comfortable being there against your wishes.'

He gazed into my eyes. The butterflies were back.

'What about your job?' he asked.

Sam sprung to mind again. I knew he needed me. I was the only one he fully opened up to. I realised I had another couple of months till the trip. Hopefully, Sam would have improved some more by then.

'I just make the tea,' I said quietly.

'What about Sam?' he asked knowingly.

I felt uncomfortable. I knew anything I said from then on would not be understood.

'He talks to me,' I explained.

Adam nodded slightly. He seemed generally interested, which surprised me.

I shrugged. 'I don't know why. I think he just needs a friend. He's very lost. I feel sorry for him. He's so lovely. You'd like him.'

Adam was still listening without judgement. 'How would you feel being away from him for so long?'

I smiled slightly. 'Does that mean you do want me to come with you?'

His sweet smile lifted my heart. The fact that his cheeks had flushed made him even more adorable.

'I do want you with me,' he said gently. 'I don't want to be anywhere without you. I can't think straight when you're not around. I love you, Mac.'

I reached forward and kissed him. I could feel his love rushing through me. I moved out of my chair to straddle him, so that I could kiss him some more. He smelled good. Shower fresh. Our morning shower filled my head. I could definitely get out of his pyjamas and back under that heavenly waterfall he had in his private bathroom.

He gently lowered my hands from his face. I could see he still had more to say.

'What about Sam?' he asked again. The question was obviously weighing heavily on his mind.

I took a steady breath. All I wanted to do was take Adam to bed, but I knew he was right. We had to finish talking about Sam.

'Sometimes, I think he needs me,' I said. 'He looks so deeply at me, as though he's known me all his life. He's so sad, Adds. He misses his wife so much. She died, and he blames himself. He breaks my heart. I just want him to heal.'

He nodded at me.

'He kissed me,' I added.

The sparkle in Adam's eyes disappeared. His body tightened. I noticed his slow and steady breaths.

'He apologised afterwards,' I said quickly. 'He didn't mean anything by it, not really.'

'What about you?' he asked. 'What did it mean to you?'

'It felt weird. Like kissing a friend.'

'We were friends. We kissed.'

I watched his eyes searching for answers. I shook my head.

'We're different. Our kiss was different. I'm not in love with Sam, I'm in love with you.'

'Can you be sure?' he asked quietly. His insecurities were shining through.

I nodded. 'I'm sure, Adds.'

He leaned forward and kissed me, making everything perfect again.

'I can't lose you, Mac,' he whispered.

'That's how I feel about you, Adds. So, if we're both on the same page, we should be all right.'

He bobbed his head slightly. 'I don't want to be jealous…'

I cut him off, ‘It’s okay. You have nothing to worry about. I love you, Adds, and that’s just the way it is, but I do care about Sam. I want him to be happy, like us. I want him to have a life too.’

‘You think you can fix him?’ he asked softly.

I shrugged. ‘Probably not.’

His hold on me tightened. ‘You’ve got a couple more months to try, Mac. If anyone can help someone, you can.’

I appreciated his attempt to show me that he trusted me. I knew he didn’t really want me anywhere near Sam, but I also knew that he wasn’t the type to stop me from being myself.

27

We had hit March, and everyone at Moreton Hall knew about my plans with Adam. Everyone except Sam. I wanted to tell him that I was preparing to leave, but I couldn't, and Victoria was against me telling Sam the truth.

She was secretly annoyed with me. I could tell. George said it was just because she was worried about how Sam would react because he was so attached to me.

I was worried as well. I didn't want my trip with Adam to be now. The timing was off, and there wasn't anything I could do about it.

There was no way I was going to watch Adam leave me behind for six months. Although, I knew we could manage it. I just didn't want us to have to.

There was just no way I could tell Sam that I would be gone from his life for six months. He was slowly coming back to life. Inch by inch, I could see the changes in him. How he smiled more. How he laughed without feeling guilty afterwards. How open he had become talking about Mindforder and Maggie.

The police had been held off. Victoria wasn't allowing a return visit from them anytime soon. Not now Sam was showing signs of improvement.

I had just cleaned up after lunch. I was having a crappy day. Sam could tell. He asked me five times over if I was all right. I lied each time. He wasn't having any of it. He was quite good at reading people, or maybe it was just me.

‘I’m not leaving this room until you tell me what’s bothering you, Mackenzie,’ he said. His voice was filled with sweetness and concern.

I sat down at the table with him. ‘I do have something I want to tell you, but I’ve been avoiding it because I don’t want to tell you.’

‘Okay, so now I’m intrigued.’ He smiled softly at me.

‘I’ve…’ I hesitated.

He nudged my arm. ‘Just spit it out, Mackenzie,’ he said gently. ‘It scares me when you hesitate. It means you’re thinking before speaking, and we both know that’s not you.’ He laughed.

I tried to hold a soft smile, but inside I could feel my heart breaking, so my smile was weak.

‘I’ve been asked to go to Europe for six months.’

There, I finally said it.

I actually felt quite relieved, for me, not him.

Sam’s eyes dropped to the table. Now he was the one with the weak smile.

‘And you’re going?’ he asked.

I nodded. ‘Yes.’

He looked up at me. ‘Who with?’

‘Adam.’

‘Your boyfriend?’

I nodded again. ‘Yes.’

‘When are you leaving?’ he asked quietly.

‘April.’

He glanced over at the window and was silent for a few minutes.

‘I plan on writing to you, every week,’ I said quickly. I hoped that might ease the blow. I didn’t want Sam to have any setbacks. Victoria wasn’t the only one who worried about that.

‘I’d like that,’ he said, still looking out the window.

I reached out and grabbed his hand. I could see that it had started to tremble. ‘I don’t want to leave you, Sam.’

He looked down at his hand in mine. ‘It will be good for you. I want you to travel. I’ll see you when you get back.’

‘You might have left by then.’

He breathed out a short laugh. ‘I doubt that, Mackenzie.’ His breathing was shallow, and his eyes were sad.

‘It’s just a little holiday,’ I said, trying to make light of it. I waved my free hand over my shoulder. ‘Won’t be that long. I’ll be back before you know it.’

He was silent.

‘I’ll call you often,’ I quickly added.

‘You shouldn’t be worried about me, Mackenzie,’ he said softly. ‘You go and enjoy yourself. I’ll be happy to read your postcards.’

‘I’ll buy you a present from every country I visit.’ I smiled his way, searching for any signs of forgiveness.

He turned to me. ‘Do you love him?’

I nodded slowly. ‘Yes.’

‘And he knows that?’

‘Yes.’

His eyes held a slight shine. ‘That’s good.’

There and then, I had to know how attached he actually was to me. ‘Do you love me, Sam?’ I blurted out.

He smiled to himself. ‘I love Maggie. You just remind me of her sometimes. It can mess with my head.’

I felt his hand slip away from mine. He stood up to leave.

‘Sam…’

He cut me off, ‘It’s all right, Mackenzie. I’m just going for a walk.’

I needed some air myself.

I waited for him to leave, and then I walked outside the side door and around to the short wall overlooking the driveway.

It was a lovely early springtime day. The birds were singing, the sun was trying to peep through the clouds, and tiny flower buds had started to sprout through here, there, and everywhere.

Moreton Hall was so much prettier in the spring. I knew Sam would be sitting by the lake, enjoying his own view. He needed some time alone, so did I, but I wasn't alone for long.

I sat on the wall and squinted my eyes down the driveway to see who it was walking towards me.

Looked like a woman.

As she got closer, I could see she looked around my age. She was slim, dark hair, pale face, and wearing jeans with a blue shirt the colour of the sky. She looked pleasant enough, but I was sure she was lost.

'Hello, can I help you?' I called out. I stood up and walked towards her before she got too close to the house.

She stopped in front of me.

I wasn't sure if I knew her. There was something familiar about her face.

'Hello,' she said politely. 'I wonder if you can help me. I'm looking for Samuel Whittington.'

My heart fell straight into the pit of my stomach. I hoped the loss of colour in my face didn't give away the lie I was about to tell.

'I'm sorry. There's no one here by that name.'

I knew what to say if anyone came calling for any of the guests. I had been well and truly trained in that area.

Her eyes weren't leaving mine at all.

'Yeah, I've heard that before,' she mumbled.

Worried thoughts rattled through my mind. Is she from Mindforder? Have they found him?

'This is private property,' I said politely. I didn't want to sound rude or come across as suspicious. 'I live here,' I added. 'I'm afraid you have the wrong address.'

She glanced down at her hand. There was a piece of paper scrunched inside her palm. 'Moreton Hall,' she said, reading her note.

I really wished George was with me.

He was in the library.

I felt the need to turn and run away, mainly to George, but my legs refused to move. My brain was telling me to act casual, play it smart, and not give out any clues.

I pointed down the driveway. 'I'll walk with you to the gate, if you like.'

My brain praised me. Yes, well done, Mac. That should do it.

She shook her head. 'Sorry, I'm not leaving until I know for sure that Sam isn't here.'

'I've already told you, there's no one here called Sam.'

'I don't believe you,' she said sharply, losing all of her politeness.

She was starting to get on my nerves.

If she thought for one moment that I was going to let her, or any of her cult friends, anywhere near him, she was highly mistaken.

'Do I need to call the police?'

She shrugged. 'Call who you like. I'm not leaving. I know he's here.'

I started to wonder what it was that she knew.

'Says who?' I demanded.

'His grandmother told me.'

I hid my surprise.

Her stern face waited for my response.

'His grandmother?' I questioned.

She nodded. 'Nana Lacey.'

I knew that was his nan's name. Surely, she wouldn't have given away Sam's safehouse.

I really needed George or Victoria to appear. One of them would have surely appeared if I were doing something stupid, or I wasn't where I was supposed to be. I needed them now, but they were inside.

I gave myself a silent pep talk. Right, that's it. I can deal with this. I've been trained. She's come here to possibly kill Sam. She'd tricked his poor old grandma, and now she thinks she's getting through me. Bring it on, girlie.

'Who are you?' I demanded.

'Maggie,' she replied quickly. 'His wife.'

I'm not sure what left my body first, my heart, my throat, my spirit, or my gumption. I froze for a moment. The birds had stopped singing, and the gentle breeze had stopped blowing. I wasn't breathing, and the clouds above me no longer moved. She shuffled a foot in the gravel, awakening me. Slowly, one by one, my senses returned.

Thoughts ran through me. She's lying. Maggie's dead. She's definitely from Mindforder, or a journalist, maybe.

'I'm going to fetch my brother to escort you off the premises, if you don't leave now,' I said, sounding just like Victoria.

She raised her eyebrows at me. 'Do what you want.'

She was stubborn and unafraid, but there was also something vulnerable about her. I could see sorrow hiding behind her cold stare. Her hands held on to the top of her brown handbag, twiddling with the seam. Her shoulders were hunched slightly, showing me she didn't have as much confidence as she pretended to have, and I could sense desperation.

She couldn't be Maggie. She just couldn't be.

I pointed out at her. 'Wait there.' My voice was filled with authority, but, to me, it felt more like nerves talking.

I practically jogged back to the house and once inside turned that powerwalk into a sprint all the way to the hunting lodge, looking for Victoria. There was no one there. I checked her office. No sign of her.

'Where the bloody hell are you?'

I ran towards the library. 'George. George,' I shouted through the hallway.

George was standing up as I swung open the library door. His face was filled with worry.

'Mac, what's happened?' He rushed towards me to peer into the hallway. 'Is it Sam?'

'It's Maggie,' I said breathlessly.

His brow furrowed. 'What?'

'She's outside, George. Standing on the driveway.' I frantically waved towards the front door. 'Maggie, George,' I repeated. 'She's out there.'

George ran towards the door and peeked outside. He looked back at me. 'Is that what she told you?'

I nodded.

'She could be one of them,' he said, scorning me as though it were my fault she was here.

'George, I think it's really her.' I gave him a knowing nod.

He examined my face for a moment. He knew I was good at knowing when people were lying.

He took another quick peek outside. He turned slowly back to me. He shook his head and frowned. 'It can't be.' He sounded just as unsure as me. He peeked again through the crack in the door. He stayed there for a minute. His face was filled with wonder when he turned back to me.

'Bloody hell, Mac,' he said, staring at me blankly. 'She looks just like you.'

I shook my head. 'No, she doesn't.'

He slowly nodded at me. 'Now, it all makes sense.'

'What does?'

'Why he's so attached to you.' He pointed at the doorway. 'She's your double.'

We both took a moment, our brains wandering off in different directions.

'Go and talk to her, George. See what you can find out,' I encouraged.

He hesitated, then gave me a slight nod. He straightened himself up and walked out the door.

I took a deep breath before heading off to follow him, but I didn't get far because George had quickly returned.

He looked worried. 'She's gone.'

28

Maggie

Please let Sam be here. That's all that ran through my mind.

His Nana Lacey had been so kind to me, and she seemed so genuine when she told me where Sam was. I believed her. It had to be true. She wouldn't have invited me into his home, shown me his pictures in frames sitting on every side, and told me he was alive, and then about Moreton Hall if it wasn't true.

I felt fed up with my journey. Ever since that raft, I had spent time in hospital, time in a mental health hospital, time at my sister's home, time travelling to Ireland, and then back to London, and now I was somewhere in Norfolk.

So much of my time spent grieving for Sam, worrying about Mindforder, and for the safety of Shane and Teddy. So much of my time wasted when I could have been searching for Sam. Alive Sam, not dead Sam's grave.

I looked around the beautiful grounds of the big posh house I had been sent to, hoping I wasn't on a wild goose chase.

It had taken me ages to convince Nana Lacey that I wasn't a fraud. At least, I thought I had convinced her, but now I wasn't so sure.

Had she really sent me here just to get me off her land? Nothing felt real anymore. Everything was one big blur from the moment Teddy told me that Sam was alive. Even that, I still wasn't sure about. I wasn't sure about anything except the fact that I needed to know the truth once and for all.

I was angry at everyone who had lied to me. From Buddy to my sister. They didn't have a right.

A breeze blew my hair and a waft of wild flowers filled the air around me, refreshing me, waking me from my trance-like walk.

Beatrix came to mind. We used to always comment on any breeze that came our way on our walks to and from the field where we'd water our husbands. We learnt how to appreciate fresh air cooling our skin.

I stopped next to a tall tree. My hand reached out and rested on the bark. I took a moment to say a silent prayer for my friend.

I opened my eyes and took a deep breath. Beatrix was waiting for me to save her. All of the women on the Island needed saving, except Joanne. She could rot in hell, if there really was such a place. I had no intention of helping her, or some of the others.

I pondered over the idea of what would happen to Mary-Lynn, Rochelle, and Guide Claris if Mindforder was brought crashing down. I hoped they got punished.

Sam's torn back washed across my mind. I remembered every time I kissed his scars, every gentle touch of his hands on my body, what he felt like, what he smelled like, and what he tasted like. I smiled at our tea and toast nights, our tee-shirt times, and that inviting look he had straight after a wash in the outside basin.

There was a lake up ahead. The edge caught my eye as I wandered across the pathway and onto the grass. I was sure someone would come for me soon to throw me off their property.

Maybe it was that woman's house. I thought that she looked a bit like me.

The top of the lake glistened as the clouds moved and the sun peeped through a gap.

My mind drifted off to the small beach where we made our rickety raft. The ocean would gleam at us, inviting us into its cool water. I had no idea it existed until Beatrix had told me. It took three weeks to find the place, and months to build our escape plan. Sneaking away most nights, using tools from Sam's place of work, and cutting up trees wore out our bodies, our minds, and our souls.

I smiled to myself, still unable to believe that we actually got away with it.

Did we? Did we get away with it? Only if Sam was truly alive.

'Please let Sam be…'

I froze. The sun disappeared behind a cloud, allowing me to widen my eyes. I stared forward to a bench in front of the lake. There was a man sitting there. He looked like…

'Sam?' I whispered, questioning my eyesight.

I knew I wished for him to be alive, so it was possible I was just seeing things.

He wasn't moving. Just looking forward. He looked slightly thinner than the Sam I knew, and his hair was shorter, but I was pretty sure it was him. It had to be.

'That is him. It can't be. Oh, come on, Maggie, get a grip. That's Sam.'

It had to be.

'Sam,' I called out.

He didn't stir.

'Sam,' I said, a little louder.

He remained motionless.

I wasn't actually sure if the words were really coming out of my mouth or if they were whirling inside of my head and I just thought I was saying them.

'Sam,' I yelled, making myself jump.

He moved. His head lifted slightly. He turned. He looked over his shoulder at me.

I froze again. My legs felt like solid lumps of concrete, and my heart was in my throat.

'Please be Sam. Please be Sam,' I muttered.

He slowly stood up and walked to the end of the bench. He tilted his head slightly to one side, as though studying me.

My mental health team had given me medication, and my sister made me take it for a while. My head felt the same dizzy swirl I used to feel when I was on those tablets.

'Sam?' I questioned loudly.

I heard a faded word float towards me. It sounded like my name.

He took a wobbly step closer to me. I found myself doing the same. There was that sound again.

'Maggie.'

My legs were moving by themselves. I was getting closer to him, and he was walking closer towards me.

The man in the dark tracksuit was almost in front of me, and there was not a person in this world who would have been able to tell me that it wasn't Sam I was looking at.

'Sam,' I confirmed. I felt the corners of my mouth lift, and my heart settle in my chest.

I couldn't believe what I was seeing. My Sam. My beautiful Sam.

'Maggie?' he questioned quietly.

His gentle eyes scanned me from head to toe. A look of confusion filled his face.

I nodded as tears entered my eyes.

His eyes glazed over too. 'They told me you were dead,' he said slowly.

'They told me that about you.'

He raised one hand to cover his mouth as tears fell down his cheeks. 'Christ, Maggie! I thought you were dead.' He flung himself forward and threw his arms around me.

I latched on as tightly as I could. I felt us both drop to our knees, as the shock no longer held us up.

Sam was sobbing into my neck. He had one hand on my back and the other on the back of my head. I could hear his gasps through my shirt.

'Oh God, Maggie,' he was saying over and over.

I moved from our hold so that I could see him. His hands instantly clasped my face, and then he started to kiss me. My mouth, my cheeks, my nose, my head, all over my face.

Our tears mingled as our faces moved around each other's. I could barely breathe. I could barely think. His sweet and salty skin tasted like home. I was home. In his arms was my only home.

'Sam,' I tried to say, but he kissed away my attempts to speak.

He grabbed a hold of my body again and held on to me as though his life depended on it.

'I can't believe this,' he whispered through sobs.

'It's all right, Sam,' I said softly. 'It's all right now.'

He moved back to look at me again. His face beamed with love, surprise, anticipation, and concern. His fingers brushed against my face.

'Maggie, is this real? I feel I'm dreaming somehow.'

I nodded. 'It's real, Sam. I'm here. We're here.'

'I don't know what to do,' he said breathlessly.

I smiled softly. 'You don't have to do anything. Just be with me now.'

His eyes smiled my way. 'Oh, I'm going to be with you, Maggie, forever. I'm never letting you out of my sight ever again.' He shook his head in disbelief that I was actually there with him.

'We're going to be okay now,' I whispered.

He nodded slightly. 'We are.'

We kissed again and again and again until we had to stop to catch our breath.

Sam's expression was still filled with amazement. He wiped away one of my falling tears. They just kept on sneaking out of my eyes.

'I love you, Maggie Whittington,' he said softly.

It was the first time he had used his last name on me. It was forbidden in Mindforder. Back there, I wasn't his, he was mine.

He nodded at me and smiled. 'Do you like that?'

I nodded and smiled back. 'I do.'

We stared at each other for a moment, both of us enjoying the view.

'Sam,' I said. 'I don't know about you, but my knees are hurting now.'

I watched the concern flash across his face. It made me smile. There he was. There was my Sam.

He slowly stood up, taking me with him. He glanced down at my jeans. 'Are you okay, Maggie?'

'Yes, Sam. I'm fine.'

He smiled at me, then gave a slight nod towards the house. 'There are some people watching us. I want you to meet them.'

I had forgotten about the house and where I was.

Sam held my hand. I knew he wasn't about to let go of me for anything or anyone.

'I especially want you to meet Mackenzie,' he told me. 'She's helped me keep my sanity around here.'

I smiled knowingly. 'The girl who looks like me?'

He nodded. 'Oh, you've seen her already?'

I looked over at the house. 'She's watching us now.'

Sam took a quick look and smiled. He turned back to me and showed me his serious face. 'I kissed her once.'

I wasn't expecting that. 'What are you trying to tell me, Sam?'

'I was thinking of you,' he said quietly, lowering his head submissively.

I used my free hand to raise his chin. 'It's okay. I understand. I forgive you. That's what you want to hear me say, isn't it?'

He nodded.

I hated it when he bowed down to me. He didn't need my forgiveness, but I knew it would make him feel better.

'Do you really love me and only me, Sam?' I asked softly, so that I didn't sound demanding.

He looked me straight in the eyes. 'It's only ever been you, Maggie. It will only ever be you. I had to tell you the truth. We said no secrets.'

I nodded. 'We did. I'm glad you told me. I love you too. It's forgotten now. Will you forget it?' I asked.

'It's gone.'

'Back to you and me now?'

He nodded and smiled.

Sam was back. I felt relieved. Now it was time to meet this Mackenzie who had helped him. I already liked her.

29

Mackenzie

'They're coming over,' I said nervously.

Victoria went over to the side door in the hunting lodge to open it, ready for Sam and Maggie.

I glanced at George. He had his serious face on. He was ready to go to work on them both.

'Hello,' said Victoria. 'You must be Maggie.'

I watched Maggie enter, followed by Sam. They were holding hands. Maggie's face was slightly flushed, and Sam looked demure. It was obvious they had both been crying.

'Hello,' said Maggie. Her voice was delicate, a touch broken. She glanced at me and George before turning her attention back to Victoria.

Victoria took charge of the awkwardness in the room. 'This is rather unexpected. You will have to excuse us if we appear at a loss for words. You have caught us off-guard.' She looked at Sam. He had his head slightly dipped. 'Sam, I'll have to make a few calls. Would you escort Maggie to the dining room.' She shot Maggie a glance. 'I'm sure she might like some tea.'

Cue me. 'We've not long finished lunch. There are some cheese sandwiches left in the fridge, if you're hungry.'

I watched Sam immediately raise his head to meet her eyes.

'Have you eaten, Maggie?' he asked softly.

'Not since breakfast,' she replied, looking at me.

Sam had his concerned face on. 'You must eat,' he told her, without it sounding demanding.

She was still watching me.

Victoria took a step forward. 'Lead the way, Sam.' She gestured towards the door.

Sam didn't move until Maggie started to make her way out of the room. He was still holding her hand but walking a slight step behind her.

We all stopped in the hallway. Victoria turned to me. 'Fetch some lunch, Mackenzie.' She turned to George and gave him a slight nod. 'George, you sit with them while I make my calls.'

George headed off in the direction of the dining room, waving Sam and Maggie towards him.

I went straight to the kitchen. I placed some cheese sandwiches on a plate, with a handful of crisps from what was left in the bowl.

George always told me not to throw away the leftover crisps, as he would snack on them throughout the day whenever he passed the kitchen.

I put the plate on a tray and grabbed three glasses and a jug from the fridge that was filled with orange juice. I made sure I didn't have a glass. I had lost my appetite for any food or drink.

My mind was blank. I just focused on the task at hand until I heard a loud scraping noise coming from the dining room. I poked my head out there to see what was going on.

George was pulling a table over to the one that Sam and Maggie were sitting at. I went back into the kitchen to fetch the tray.

George was explaining some things about Moreton Hall as I placed the tray down on his table.

Sam reached out and took the plate and put it straight in front of Maggie.

I could see they were still holding hands.

He gave her a look that she seemed to understand. Using her free hand, she picked up half of the sandwich. Sam's eyes never left her face until she took the first bite. His shoulders relaxed, and his mouth softened.

George leaned closer to the table. 'You know Victoria will be calling your mum now, and Lennie, to name a few,' he said to Sam.

Sam nodded. 'That's okay. They all need to know.'

George waited for Maggie to swallow her food. 'Where are you staying, Maggie?'

'I have a room in a hotel in a small town up the road, Breanstone,' she replied.

Sam smiled at me. 'It has a cute model railway village.'

She nodded. 'I think I saw a sign.'

I stared down at Maggie's crisps as she continued to eat.

'Just so we're clear,' said George, 'you won't be able to stay here with Sam.'

Sam's smile disappeared immediately. 'I'm not leaving Maggie,' he said flatly.

George wasn't done talking. 'Maggie, I'm sorry, but Sam is in our care. There are steps in place. We have procedures.'

Maggie nodded. She seemed understanding.

Sam wasn't about to agree. 'I no longer need care,' he told George. 'I'm fine now.'

George held a sympathetic smile. 'Sam, you have been through a great trauma.' He glanced at Maggie. 'You too. We have to be sure that Sam's mental health is stable.'

'I'm stable,' he said adamantly.

'I only want what is best for Sam,' she said, smiling sweetly. 'I haven't come here to disrupt anything. I just had to find him.'

Sam looked to me, as though pleading for my help.

I turned to George. 'I think Sam's going to be all right now.' I felt Maggie's eyes on me before I even looked.

'Thank you for helping him,' she said to me.

Sam was more focused on George. 'I'm going to leave with Maggie. I'm going home with my wife.'

'Do you have a home?' George questioned her.

She shook her head.

Sam cut in, 'I'll buy us a home. We'll have a home.'

His hand tightened on hers.

'You're both still in danger, you know that,' said George.

There was a moment of silence, then George got up.

'I'll speak to Victoria. See if Maggie can stay a couple of days while we sort things out, but you know this is a private home, Sam.'

That was George's polite way of saying that guests had to pay to stay.

Sam was looking directly at George. 'Maggie can afford to stay here.'

Maggie didn't look so sure.

George nodded and left the room.

I suddenly felt vulnerable. All eyes were on me. I didn't have any answers, but it seemed Maggie had things she wanted to say.

'Sam, I don't have any money,' she whispered.

I tried to lean away from them as far as I could go. I was pretty sure Maggie wouldn't want me involved in their conversation.

Sam's face was filled with warmth as he looked at her. 'You're my wife, Maggie. My money is yours.'

There was a slight awkward silence. Her hand was twiddling a crisp.

Sam leaned closer to her. 'Don't worry, we have more than enough to stay here,' he whispered.

I didn't know why they kept whispering. I could hear everything quite clearly. I was right there.

Maggie stopped playing with her food. 'Sam, what are we going to do about Beatrix?'

The colour in Sam's face faded.

'I can't move on with my life knowing she's waiting on me to save her,' she told him.

Sam was silent.

Maggie gave a gentle tug on his hand. 'Sam, will you help me?'

'I'll do whatever you want me to do, Maggie,' he said reluctantly.

'Won't that be dangerous?' I asked.

She nodded. 'We have no choice. People are suffering. Buddy needs stopping.'

I understood, but I also knew that Sam needed to be away from that life, not brought back into it.

'I'm not sure Sam's ready to take on Mindforder,' I said, looking for his reaction to my interference.

His head lowered, along with his voice. 'I'll do what Maggie needs me to do.'

'I just want Sam to be safe,' I said quickly.

Her eyes shot to mine. 'So do I, but I can't walk away from this.'

I turned to Sam. 'Perhaps Maggie could speak to that officer who came here.' I looked over at her. 'The people who own this place are connected to a team of police who deal specifically with cult crimes.'

She looked hopeful. 'That would be a great start.'

Sam didn't look as sure, but he offered her a weak smile.

George entered the room. He called over to us, 'Maggie can stay.' He looked her way. 'I'll drive you back to your hotel to collect your things.'

Sam's body shifted. 'Don't leave, Maggie,' he whispered to her.

'I'll go,' I said, standing. 'Just give me your room key, Maggie, and I'll sort it out for you.'

Sam's eyes smiled my way.

Maggie rummaged through her bag and pulled out a key. She told me the name of the hotel. I knew it well. Uncle Bert's wife was the owner's cousin. It was a small town. There was hardly any escape from family members.

'I won't be long.' I took the key and walked out to the hallway. They followed me. Sam brought the plate of food with him.

Victoria came out of her office. 'Sam,' she said, looking at Maggie. 'Take Maggie to your room. I'm sure she needs a rest. Lennie will be here in a couple of hours. We'll talk then.'

Sam lowered his head, turned towards the stairs, and then waited for Maggie to lead him.

I watched her nudge him forward, and I heard her whisper, 'Walk beside me, Sam.'

* * *

George was driving at his usual slow pace, which was getting quite annoying because I wanted to hurry up and get back to Sam. I saw the sign for Breanstone, and smiled to myself.

'I have never experienced anything like this before, Mac.'

'That's because people don't tend to come back from the dead, George.'

'I don't even know what's going to happen next,' he admitted.

I shrugged. 'I guess they live happily ever after.'

George shook his head. 'They've got a fight on their hands with Mindforder first.'

'I hope they don't fight them. I don't want Sam to be in danger.'

'They'll probably get put in witness protection, Mac.'

'He's protected now.'

George pulled into the hotel's small car park. We got out of his car and crunched our way over the gravel, heading for the main door.

'I'll sort the paperwork with Dora while you make a start in Maggie's room,' he told me.

We entered the chalky white building shaped like a small castle.

Dora was surprised to see us at first. Her long, slim face showed signs of worry. She thought we had come with bad news.

George explained our visit, as best he could under the circumstances.

Dora gave me the go ahead, so I went off to find Maggie's room.

The first thing I did was sit down on the bed in the small Laura Ashley styled room. I felt emotionally drained. My phone vibrated in my pocket. I had a feeling it was Adam with his latest itinerary plans.

Between him and Malorie, I had my trip to Europe all planned out. Every single moment. It was starting to feel exhausting. The only good part would be the allocated alone time I would spend with Adam. I was looking forward to that part. I knew that we had to work around the exhibition, but I wasn't expecting a tight schedule around other stuff that, in my opinion, didn't matter.

I reluctantly looked at my phone.

It was Adam.

I slumped.

'Oh please, Adam. I can't take any more holiday lists. Not now. I feel tired. I wish you were here, holding me. I just want to feel your arms around me,' I mumbled to the room.

I took a deep breath and started to read his message…

I see magic all around you
In every vision and in sound
Take a breath and rest awhile
You're safe, you have been found.

In every passing season
I'll be right by your side
I love you, Mackenzie Watson
And that love will never die.

My hand flopped against my chest. 'Oh, Adds, how lovely.' I smiled as a surge of energy lifted my spirits.

30

Maggie

Snuggling into Sam's body, lying on his bed, felt surreal. It wasn't our bed. We no longer had a bed. We no longer had anything but each other. I smiled at his sweatshirt. It seemed so strange. Everything was strange. Everything was so different, except his arms around me. His hold was familiar.

I shuffled my head along his chest until I was looking up at his face. His warm eyes were waiting for me.

'I'll get us a home, Maggie. We'll have a place where we belong.'

He always could read my mind.

He smiled. 'You can pick whatever one you want.'

I reached up and stroked his face. 'I wish we were in our own home now.'

His smile widened. 'Why, what do you want to do?'

I leant up to rest on my elbow. 'Who says I want to do anything?' I asked innocently.

'Your face says.'

My grin was just as wide as his. 'I can't help it if I want my husband.'

'Your husband wants you too.'

'What you going to do about it?'

He breathed out a laugh, sat up, and rolled me on my back.

There was so much love in his eyes shining my way. My heart melted. I was lost in him, with his strange clothes and new bed. Nothing mattered but him.

'What do you want me to do?' he asked softly.

I bit my lip and tried not to laugh. 'Everything.'

He laughed at me, then looked over his shoulder at the bedroom door.

'You really want to do it here?' he asked.

I shrugged. 'Lock the door.'

He smiled. 'It doesn't have a lock.'

'Oh great!'

He laughed and sat up. 'What do you want to do, Maggie?'

'I want us to be naked under these covers.'

'You sure?'

I matched his mischievous grin and nodded into the pillow.

He reached out his hands, took mine, and lifted me from the bed. I stumbled forward into his chest. His familiar scent hit my nose. I breathed him in. His arms rolled down the sleeves of my shirt, then they came up to slowly unbutton my top.

I took a deep breath when he reached the bottom. I waited for him to pull his top over his head. He let it drop to the floor behind him. His head lowered until his face met mine. Our cheeks brushed.

My shirt was draped down over the back of my shoulders, then it joined the sweatshirt on the carpet. Sam's lips were on my skin, gently kissing where my shoulder met my neck. I closed my eyes for a second to log every touch.

Sam started to take off my jeans. I helped once they sat at my ankles. He gently removed my socks and kissed my knees while he was down there.

I waited for him to remove his bottoms before I took off my underwear. He leaned over me to flip back the covers on the bed.

I climbed in, quickly followed by him. We snuggled down, with me beneath him.

His eyes were focused on mine.

'Are you sure, Maggie?' he asked quietly.

I blinked slowly. 'I've missed you, Sam.'

'I've missed you too, but Victoria could walk in at any moment.'

'That's her problem.'

He laughed quietly. 'Well, it'll be something for her to put in her notes.'

I reached up and held his face. His grin turned to a warm smile that matched his glazed eyes.

'Mr Whittington,' I teased. 'Your wife is waiting.'

He laughed. 'Oh, is she?'

I closed my eyes as his face lowered towards me. We were home.

* * *

I stepped out of the bathroom, fresh from the shower, fresh from more time spent with Sam, to find my belongings in his bedroom. I was pleased to put on some different clothes. I glanced to my scrunched garments on the floor and smiled. I guessed Mackenzie had seen them too.

Sam looked over my shoulder at my small suitcase.

'You don't have a lot of things.'

I turned to him and smiled cheekily. 'Got you, that's all I need.'

I could see that my words warmed him. His cheeks flushed slightly. He put his arms around me and kissed my head.

'We had better get dressed and face the music,' I mumbled into his bare chest.

He looked down at me. 'I don't care what they say, Maggie. We're getting out of here. We're going to live our lives.'

I took a step back. 'I want that too. A house in the country, far away from anywhere, so when it's dark, all we can see are the stars.'

He nodded. 'Sounds good to me.'

I stopped smiling. 'But first, we have to help Beatrix. I want to speak to the cult police.'

He breathed out a short laugh. 'The cult police?'

I shrugged. 'Whatever they're called. They can help Beatrix. I'm going to give them all the information they need.'

He nodded, pulled his towel off his waist, and wiped his face with one corner. 'Okay.'

'I know you don't want to do this.'

'I don't,' he admitted, 'but I will, for you.'

I stepped forward and placed my hand on his arm. 'I'm scared, Sam.' He needed to know everything I was feeling. I didn't want to pretend to be strong when everything inside of me was hanging on by a thread.

He nodded. 'So am I, Maggie. That's why I don't want you involved.'

'But we are involved, Sam.'

'Yeah,' he mumbled to himself, turning away to get dressed.

* * *

Mackenzie was the only one in the hallway. I think she was waiting for us. I noticed Sam's face light up when he saw her. She held the same expression.

'Sam,' she greeted.

'Thank you, Mackenzie, for getting Maggie's stuff,' he said softly.

It was clear they had a bond. Their body language and tone towards each other were locked.

I gave her the once over. She really did look like me.

I smiled to myself. I could see why Sam was taken with her. I moved my fingers slightly in his hand to remind him I was there.

He glanced down at my hand. 'Where is everyone?' he asked Mackenzie.

She nodded over towards a dark-wood door. 'Victoria's office. Lennie's inside, and your mum is due here tomorrow morning.'

Sam raised his eyebrows. 'Joy,' he mumbled.

Mackenzie clasped her hands together tightly. 'They're talking about inviting the cult police back here again to talk to Maggie.'

'Cult police,' said Sam, eyeing me sideways. He laughed to himself.

She shrugged. 'It's a good name for them.'

'Maggie wants to talk with them,' he told her.

She looked at me. She looked worried. She wasn't the only one.

'You can tell them in a minute,' she said, mainly to Sam.

There was a moment of silence. No one seemed to know what to say next.

'How are you, Sam?' she asked gently. 'You know, with everything?'

He glanced at me, then at her. 'Erm… it's been a bit of a weird day.'

She nodded.

So did I.

He cleared his throat. 'Not too sure how I feel at the moment.'

I looked at the floor. I had nothing to add. Inside, I agreed with him.

'You're going to heal now,' she said gently.

I started to feel like I wasn't there.

He gazed over at her. 'Yeah, I think I might.'

She smiled warmly at him, and he returned the gesture.

'Thank you, Mackenzie,' he said, sounding like it was the last time he would speak to her.

The door to Victoria's office opened and she stepped out to greet us. Sam immediately told her that I wanted to talk to the police. She nodded and waved us inside, leaving Mackenzie alone again in the hallway.

31

Mackenzie

The garden umbrella shaded me from the strong sunlight shining all around. I smiled at the refreshing breeze that swept over me, lifting the smell of sunscreen from my skin. I looked ahead to admire the vast landscape around me. There were mountains in the distance on one side, and a vineyard on the other that stretched down towards a rustic cream house with a yellow roof.

I turned my head to watch Adam doing lengths in the outdoor swimming pool to the right of the patio table I was sitting at. He looked as gorgeous as ever.

We had been in the north-east of Spain for two weeks. So far, it was my favourite stopover. The house we were staying in was huge, white, and rather empty on the furniture front. Not that we cared. We didn't spend a lot of time looking at the décor.

It was June, it was hot, we were somewhere beautiful, and we were together. That's all I cared about, and Adam hadn't stopped smiling since we boarded Jack's private plane.

Malorie had joined us on the first flight, which was to Paris. She told us she had business there, but Adam wasn't buying any of it.

She had given me a camera on the short journey and a small red laptop. I was asked to record differences between women in each country, and to take pictures.

Malorie had a friend who worked for a magazine that I hadn't heard of, and the editor had agreed to do an article from my findings.

I was quite scared. What did I know about journalism?

I wasn't sure what Malorie expected of me. She had told me that it would be educational for me, and Adam just gave me a sympathetic smile at the time.

I glanced down at my laptop. I wasn't writing anything about women of the world, or rather, Europe. I was about to type up an email to George to give to Sam.

Sam and Maggie, as far as I knew, were still at Moreton Hall. George had kept me informed about their journey all the way through mine. I shared everything with Adam about Sam's incredible reunion with his wife, and the truth about Moreton Hall.

Adam knew I had signed a privacy agreement, but Sam was making the news, and I had been following the story whenever I could. Moreton Hall was kept out of it, but Victoria knew that Adam knew of Sam, so she had a non-disclosure agreement sent to him. He also knew I was writing to Sam, and he was fine with that.

I removed my sunglasses and wiped away some creases that had formed on the lap of my pink sundress. I looked back at the screen to read over Sam's last email to me.

> Hello, Mackenzie. We loved your last postcard. You've made Maggie want to see the world now. Hopefully, we will soon, now that Buddy has been arrested.
>
> Beatrix is safe and has returned to England. We might be able to see her again one day, but not till after the trial. I know you've been following the news whenever you can, so you know most of what is going on.
>
> They're saying that Bluebird is not in a good mental state of mind to testify at the moment, so it's just some

of us past and present members who will be going to court.

Maggie has been so strong throughout. I've just pretty much been me. Well, you know what a mess I can be.

I have these thoughts, Mackenzie. I visualise us all together in a happy place. I hope it comes true one day. Victoria told me she sent Adam a non-disclosure agreement so that you can tell him about Moreton Hall, and the truth about me, which is good news. I'd like for us to meet Adam, and to see you again, of course. I miss your goofy grin.

I know I keep saying it, but I like saying it, thank you for being my friend.

I hope you're having the best time in Europe. I look forward to reading what you have to say next and finding out where you are.

By the way, my mum has really taken to Maggie. I think it helped when Maggie told her that she'd like us to live in Ireland when all of this is over.

Speak to you soon, Mackenzie. Take care now, and no more drunken wheelchair rides. You're lucky you didn't break something other than the chair. I'm glad Adam's mum sorted out a replacement.

Make sure you're eating properly, and stay out of the swimming pools. How many times has that lad got to save you!

Love, Sam.
Maggie says hi.

I laughed to myself and turned to the swimming pool. How was I supposed to know that the pool in Paris had a wave machine. Paddling in shallow ends for me from now on. I glanced at Adam's wheelchair over by the back doors of the house. I was permanently banned for sitting in the NASA built contraption.

Most people have normal wheelchairs, not ones with rocket-launch gadgets that nosedive you at 30mph across a field. At least I learnt how to do a professional stunt roll.

Adam and the pool looked inviting. I got up and made my way over to its edge, shallow end, and plonked myself down. I scrunched my dress up to the top of my thighs and dangled my bare legs in the cool water, admiring my suntan.

Adam swam towards me and stopped in front of me. He rested his hands on my legs and kissed the side of my knee.

I smiled down at him, then slid my body into the water. He had one hand holding the edge of the pool, and the other holding me. I wrapped myself around him and used my legs to pull him closer to me.

'You know you and swimming pools don't mix,' he said playfully.

'I'm getting your attention,' I teased.

He grinned his lovely cute grin that got me every time without fail.

'I know that some people might be against the idea,' he said, sounding warm and serious at the same time, 'but I want to ask you if you'd…'

'Yes, I'll marry you.'

He laughed. 'I wasn't going to ask that. I was going to ask if you wanted to move in with me when we got home.'

'Oh!'

His face was filled with curiosity. He moved back slightly to read my expression. 'Do you want to get married, Mac?'

I shrugged, trying to wave off my embarrassment. I could feel my cheeks reddening, and it wasn't because of the hot sun belting down on us.

He asked me again. This time without the humour.

'I would like to,' I said quietly.

'Okay.' He came closer to my body. 'Then, that's what we'll do.'

I grinned. 'People will say we haven't been together long.'

He smiled. 'Mac, we've been together all our lives.'

And that was another of my life-changing moments and, to date, my favourite.

If you enjoyed this book, why not check out this contemporary romance with a fantasy twist by K.T. Dady…

A Thousand Years

Printed in Great Britain
by Amazon

13917817R00150